Edmund Yates

Broken to harness

Vol. II

Edmund Yates

Broken to harness
Vol. II

ISBN/EAN: 9783337138462

Printed in Europe, USA, Canada, Australia, Japan

Cover: Foto ©Andreas Hilbeck / pixelio.de

More available books at **www.hansebooks.com**

BROKEN TO HARNESS

A Story of English Domestic Life

BY

EDMUND YATES

"Mit dem Gürtel, mit dem Schleier,
Reisst der schöner Wahn entzwei."

IN THREE VOLUMES

VOL. II.

THIRD EDITION

LONDON

JOHN MAXWELL AND COMPANY

122 FLEET STREET

M DCCC LXIV.

LONDON:

ROBSON AND SON, GREAT NORTHERN PRINTING WORKS,
Pancras Road, N.W.

CONTENTS OF VOL. II.

BROKEN TO HARNESS.

CHAPTER I.

MINING OPERATIONS.

No sooner was the Churchills' wedding safely over than all further reason for keeping on the establishment at Bissett Grange was at an end, and the party broke up at once. Sir Marmaduke went straight to Paris, and took up his quarters at Meurice's, according to his annual custom, to the disgust of Gumble, who detested all things "forring" with that pious horror always to be found in the British serving-class. The old gentleman knew Paris better perhaps than he knew London, and was thoroughly well known in the best circles of Parisian society; his eccentricity, *quelque chose bizarre*, which distinguished him from the ordinary run of English visitors, made him popular with the young people, while his perfectly polished manner to women, the unmistakable not-to-be-acquired high-breeding of the true gentleman, combined with his ready wit and biting sarcasm, both expressed in perfect French, rendered him a favourite with his coevals. To the Faubourg and its inhabitants, however, his visits were principally confined; he had never yielded allegiance to the Imperial Court, and used to speak of it and its august head in a very disparaging manner. " Gad, sir!" he would say in the smoke-room of Meurice's, after his return from the Français or from some grand reception,—" Gad, sir! I've a very low opinion of your what d'ye call him?— your Emperor! met him often when he was in England,—at Gore House, and two or three other places; always found him a silent, moody, stupid fellow—that's it! a stupid fellow, by Jove!— tries to make out that he holds his tongue to think the more; like the monkey, you know. My belief is, that he's so deuced quiet because he's got nothing to say. And his surroundings, my dear fellow! his surroundings, awful! De Rossignol, who was a billiard-marker or a singer at a *café chantant*, or something of that kind; Oltenhaus, the financier, who is a Polish Jew, of the worst stamp; and O'Malley, the Marshal, a mere Irish adventurer! That is not the sort of stuff for Courts, sir!—the sweepings of the Boulevard theatres, the Juden-Gasse at Frankfort, and the long-sword, saddle, bridle, whack-fol-de-rol, and all the rest of it, of the bold dragoon! *Vieille école bonne école* is a good maxim, by Jove! They mayn't be clever; but they're gentle-people at least, and that's not saying a little for them!"

So the old gentleman growled to the little select circle round him, enjoying himself meanwhile in the highest degree. Perhaps one of the most gratifying results of his sojourn in Paris he could not have explained, though at the time he was, however unconsciously, keenly sensible of it; it was that he had Gumble at his mercy. So desolate, so bored, so completely used up was that great man, that he looked forward to the time of his master's retiring for the night, and getting up in the morning, as the only two happy periods in his Parisian existence. All the toilet-ceremonies, before held by him in deep disgust, were now lingered over with the utmost fondness, and every scrap of gossip was brought forward in the chance of its provoking a discussion, and protracting the period when the valet should be again relegated to the company of the French and German waiters and pert ladies'-maids, who scoffed at Gumble's old-fashioned ways and stories. Of course there were other gentlemen's gentlemen installed with their masters at Meurice's; but they were all much younger than Gumble; and when their "governors" were not expected home till late, beguiled the weary hours with pleasant dances at the Salle Valentino, or such-like resorts. But Gumble was a little too old, and a great deal too insular, to enjoy these recreations. Once indeed he had been persuaded into attending one of these public balls; but the sight of his deep white choker, straight-brushed whiskers, and solemn old mug, had such an effect on the dancers,—Jules utterly missing his great bound in the *cavalier seul*, and Eulalie failing to touch her *vis-à-vis* shoulder with her toe in the *en avant deux*,—that he was requested to confine his *tristesse* to some other place; and as he was really not amused, he willingly consented. So, after that, he remained at Meurice's, generally sitting solitary in a crowd of chattering French servants, beguiling the time sometimes by speculating how long his master would live, and what he would leave him at his death; whether a green-grocer's or a public-house would be the most profitable business to undertake with Sir Marmaduke's legacy; whether he could get any thing for the recipe of some wonderful boot varnish which he alone possessed; sometimes by reading a shilling novel of fashionable life, or nodding dreamily over the *Times* of the previous day. One night, as he was attending his master to bed, he brought forth a special bit of news which he had reserved.

"House full here, sir," said he, as he was mixing the old gentleman's evening draught.

"Ah!" growled Sir Marmaduke. "God bless my soul, pack of people come over by the rail devilish cheap, and all that sort of thing. Poor dear old diligences kept the place clear; that was one comfort. Full, eh? Any body I know?"

"Capting Currer, from the Forring Office, come in to-night, sir; saw he had a white shammy-leather bag with him, sir—"

"Ah! Queen's messenger off to-morrow morning to Smyrna or Kamschatka, or some infernal place. Any body else?"

"Miss Lexden come, sir; but we was full here, just full; so she have gone next door to the Windsor, sir. Only Withers with her, sir; no one else. Must miss Miss Barbara, sir—Mrs. Churchill, sir—I shouldn't think, sir."

"What the devil business is it of yours? What right have you to think about it? There now; be off! Good night."

"Bless my soul!" said the old gentleman, when he was left alone. "I'm deuced glad Susan didn't get in here, or she'd have led me a pretty life. I suppose I must call on her to-morrow morning. Deuced unpleasant talk there'll be—Barbara, and all the rest of it. Poor girl! Susan

—too hard—come round at last;" and musing in this way Sir Marmaduke fell asleep.

When, in the course of the next day, he called upon Miss Lexden, he found that lady in the highest spirits. "I knew you were here, Sir Marmaduke," said she. "I've had Cabanel here;— you recollect little Cabanel? Spanish-looking little fellow with black eyes; was an attaché when the Walewskis were in London;—and he saw you at the duchess's last week. You're going there to-morrow of course? How well you look! that's the climate, you know, and the style of life; so much better than in that wretched old island of ours."

"What news do you bring from that wretched old island of ours?" asked the old gentleman.

"News? none; not a scrap, positively not a scrap; nobody in town, not a soul. I didn't wait there above a day, but came through at once."

"You did not stop long enough to see the Churchills, I suppose?"

"The— eh? I beg your pardon, I did not catch the name."

" The Churchills."

" Churchills !" echoed Miss Lexden, with the greatest deliberation; " Churchills! I have not the least idea who you mean."

" Ah !" said Sir Marmaduke, through his closed teeth. " No, of course not; you don't recollect your own brother's child, even when there's no one in town. If it had been in the season, I could not have attempted to suggest any thing so horribly low; but I thought perhaps, that when there was not a soul in town, as you said, you might have thought of the girl who is of your blood, and who has been, as it were, your daughter for ten years." And the old gentleman stamped his stick on the floor, and looked fiercely across at his cousin.

" O—h !" said Miss Lexden, perfectly calmly. " I didn't follow you at first; now I see. It seems strange to me that a man with your knowledge of the world, Marmaduke Wentworth,—more especially with your knowledge of me, derived in times past, when you had full opportunity of making yourself acquainted with my character,—should have imagined that I should for an instant have altered in my purpose as regards my niece Barbara. What is there to induce me to swerve one atom from—"

" What?" interrupted Sir Marmaduke; "what? Old age, Susan Lexden! You and I are two old people, who ought to be thankful to have been left here so long; and not to bear malice and all sorts of miserable hatred in our old age, more especially to our own kindred. You're vexed with Barbara, not unnaturally, as you'd set your heart upon seeing her married to a rich man; but that's over now, and so make the best of it. Her husband's a good fellow and a gentleman; so what more do you want?"

" What more !" exclaimed the old lady; " what more ! Freedom from this style of conversation; permission to go my own way without comment or impertinent suggestion. I use the adjective advisedly; I claim my right to visit those whom I like, to ignore those whom I dislike, without such remarks from those who I distinctly say have no right to make them. And, however old I may be, I am not yet sufficiently in my dotage to show affection, kindness, no, nor even recognition, to those who have wilfully disregarded my desires."

So Sir Marmaduke retired worsted from the conflict, and contented himself with writing a letter to Major Stone, bidding that worthy take the first opportunity of a visit to town to ascertain how Churchill and Barbara were getting on.

Mr. Beresford, after leaving Bissett, went for a short visit to a bachelor friend with a shooting-box in Norfolk; and after enjoying some excellent sport, and nearly boring himself to death, in the company of his host and a few hard-drinking sporting squires of the neighbourhood, returned to town — to his lodgings in South Audley Street, and to his daily routine of life. He did not at all dislike London in the autumn, when he had no calls to make; when he could wear out his old clothes; could smoke in the streets at any hour without loss of dignity; could get a little quiet reading and a little quiet play-going; and need not fear the admonitory missives of duns, who concluded that all their customers were, or ought to be, out of town at that dull season. Moreover, he had not spent all of the last two hundred pounds he had borrowed, and had received his October quarter's salary; so that, on the whole, he was in very good case, and came smiling radiantly into Simnel's room on the first morning after his return. Mr. Simnel, as usual, had a pile of papers before him; but he pushed them aside at Beresford's entrance; rose up, welcomed him; and placing his back against the mantel-piece, at once entered into conversation.

"Well, Mr. Commissioner," he commenced; "so you've got back to the hive, eh? and now I suppose you mean to remain, and let one of the other hard-worked members of the Board have a little rest, eh?"

"Yes," replied Beresford; "I'm a fixture now for a long time; I must take to the collar, and stick to it; but you, old fellow,—do you mean to say you've been here all this blessed time?"

"I've not moved away yet," said Simnel; "some one must do the work, you know," he added with a meaning grin.

"Yes, I know, of course; and a deuced hard grind you've had of it.   But you'll go away now, I suppose?"

"No; I shall run down to Leicestershire and get a little hunting next month perhaps; that is, if I can get away; and I might take a fortnight in Paris at Christmas, just to avoid the 'God bless yous!' and 'Happy years!' and other jackass congratulations, which I hate and abominate."

"Genial creature!" said Beresford, regarding him with great complacency; "what's the news?"

"That's just what I should ask you," retorted Simnel; "there's no news here. Sir Hickory has been to the Lakes, and 'my lady' was much pleased with Ullswater; which is more, I should think, than Ullswater was with 'my lady,' always supposing Ullswater to have any taste. Old Peck has slept as much as usual; but has not devoted

as much time as he generally does to his get-up,
and has consequently been rather red and rusty
about his beard. O'Scanlon has been dying for
your return, that he may get away; and the men
in the Office are just the same as ever. Oh, by
the way, I see that marriage has come off?"

"Which marriage?"

"That man Churchill, who was staying with
you at old Wentworth's, has married that dashing
girl—what was her name?—Lexden!"

"Yes; and the *other* marriage has come off.
Old Schröder is one flesh now with Miss Townshend; that's a nice thing to think of, isn't
it?"

"Ay, I heard of that too; saw it in the paper
of course; but beyond that, one of the young
fellows here, Pringle, had cards; he's a connexion, or something of the sort."

"Yes; they've taken a thundering big house
in Saxe Coburg Square,—in the new South Kens-
ington district, you know,—and are coming out
heavily. There's a dinner there on Thursday, to
which I'm asked; and a reception afterwards.

It's a bad time of year; but there *may* be some new fillies trotted out, you know."

"Ah! you've done nothing more in that matter, I suppose? no one on hand just now? no combination of money and beauty, as Jack Palmer says, when he rides with Schwarzchild into the City?"

"None! I've had no chance; but I should think this wouldn't be a bad opening. They are a tremendously well-tinned set at Schröder's; and he's safe to ask no women who are not enormously ingotted. With such girls, unaccustomed to any thing but what was Paddington and is now Tyburnia, one might have a chance, for they've seen nothing decent yet, you know. Your stockbrokering gent is a hopeless beast!" And Mr. Beresford shrugged his shoulders, and then looked down at his feet, as though Capel Court lay beneath them.

"You're going to the dinner?" asked Simnel.

"Going, my dear fellow! if you had been staying for the last month, as I have, with Jim Coverdale, you wouldn't ask the question. No better fellow than Jim breathes, and there's always capital sport to be got at his place; but the cooking is something indescribably atrocious. One always feels inclined, when he asks you what you'd like for dinner, to use the old *mot*, and say, ' *Chez vous, monsieur, on mange, mais on ne dine pas.*' After a month's experience of Coverdale's cook, I am looking forward with eager anticipation to the performances of such an artist as Schröder will probably employ."

"I should think," said Mr. Simnel, after a minute's pause—"I should think it probable that Mr. Townshend will be there."

"First dinner after his daughter's marriage," said Beresford. "Duty, by Jove! Of course he will."

"If he is there, I want you to do me a favour," said Simnel, quietly.

"And that is—?" asked Beresford, in whose ears the word 'favour' always rang with a peculiar knell.

"A very slight one, and involving very little trouble to you; else, you may take your oath, I know you too well to expect you'd grant it," said Simnel, with some asperity. "No! I merely want you, in the course of conversation, and when you have fully secured Mr. Townshend's attention, to introduce, no matter how, the name of a firm--- Pigott and Wells."

"Pigott and Wells!" repeated Beresford, mechanically.

"Pigott and Wells. Should he ask you anything further, you will remember that it is the name of a cotton firm in Combcardingham; and take care that it fits into your story. That's all!"

"It won't get me into any row, will it?" asked the cautious commissioner; "you're such a tremendously sly old *diplomate*, such an infernal old Machiavel, that I am always afraid of your getting me into a mess."

"Sweet innocent! you need not fear. There's no harm in the name. Of course it depends upon yourself how you bring it in."

And Mr. Beresford, with a vivid recollection of owing eight hundred pounds to Mr. Simnel, undertook the commission.

About the same time Mr. Schröder's domestic arrangements were being discussed under the same roof, in No. 120.

"What are you going to do on Thursday night, Jim?" asked Mr. Pringle of Mr. Prescott.

"Nothing," said Mr. Prescott.

"Then don't," said Mr. Pringle. "It don't answer and it don't pay. I've got a card for a party in Saxe Coburg Square, and I'll take you if you like to come."

"But I don't like to come. I'm sick of all your parties, with the same grinning and bowing nonsense, the same bosh talked, the same wretched routine from first to last. Who are the people?"

"Now, what a duffer you are!" said Mr. Pringle; "first you declaim in the strongest virtuous indignation against all parties, and then you ask who the people are! Well; they are connexions of mine. Old Townshend, my godfather, who's an old beast, and who never gave me any thing except a tip of half-a-crown once when I was going to school, has married his daughter—deuced pretty girl she is too—to a no-end rich City party—

Schröder by name. And Mrs. Schröder is 'at home' on Thursday evening, 'small and early;' and I've got a card, and can take you. There's a dinner-party first, I hear; but I am not asked to that."

"What a pity!" said Prescott; "your true philosopher only goes to dinners. Balls and receptions are well enough when one is very young; but they soon pall. There is in them an insincere glitter, a spurious charm, which—"

"Yes, thank ye," interrupted Mr. Pringle; "for which see *Pelham passim*, or the collected works of the late Lord Byron. Much obliged; but I subscribe to Mudie's; and would sooner read the sentiments in the original authors. What I want to know is, whether you'll come?"

"No, then."

"Yes, you will. I know you, you old idiot, and all the reason for your moping,—as hough that would advance the cause one bit. Yes, you will. We'll dine at Simpson's; have a quiet weed in my chambers; dress there; and go into the vortex together."

CHAPTER II.

THE SCHRÖDERS AT HOME.

MR. BERESFORD was thoroughly well-informed when he announced Miss Townshend's marriage with M. Gustav Schröder. That event took place almost immediately after the break-up of the party at Bissett Grange, and Sir Marmaduke attended it on his way through to Paris. The wedding was a very grand affair, and created quite a sensation in the dead time of the year. A bishop, who in his private capacity held some land which he had sold to a railway company numbering Mr. Townshend among its directors, was entrapped for the ceremony, which, of course, took place at St. George's, Hanover Square. There was such a gathering of carriages, and such a champing and stamping of horses in George Street, that two men who were sleeping at Limmer's, on their way through town, were ac-

tually induced to shake off dull sloth so early as
eleven A.M., and to peer out of the window at the
cavalcade; satisfying themselves with a very short
glance, however, and returning to their couches
again with great alacrity. Very great magnates
in the banking world, the brokering world, the
colonial-export world, and the shipping world, were
present; as were M. Heinrich Schröder, repre-
sentative of the house at Frankfort, a bent shriv-
elled old gentleman, with marked Jewish profile;
thin hands always plucking at his thin lips, and a
very small knowledge of the English language;—
M. Louis Schröder, who represented the house at
Paris, a man of forty, short, stout, genial, and jolly;
speaking all languages with equal ease; with a
keen eye for making money, but enjoying nothing
better than spending it; drinking very little, but
fond of high-living and high-play; and showing
general sensuality in his thick scarlet lips and short
pudgy hands; more Schröders, male and female,
from Hamburg, from Mainz, from Florence; and
one—very much burnt up—who had just returned
from losing his liver, and gaining his fortune at

Ceylon. Mr. Townshend contributed the eminent personages in City firms above mentioned, but none of his family were present; and it was remarked by some of the guests, that none of his family had ever been seen by any body,—any body meaning, of course, any body in their society; but, owing to its being the dull season of the year, Miss Townshend's list was not as brilliant as it might have been. For instance, ever since as a child she married her doll to a resplendent individual in a soft scarlet-cloth coat, a cocked hat, and a pair of linen trousers (supposed to be of the male sex, but really another doll in disguise, as proved by the lump of painted hair projecting behind), she had always intended having eight bridesmaids; but Clara Hamilton and Kate Brandon were away with their people, and in their places she had asked the Melville girls, to whom, as she afterwards found, her trump card, her prettiest bridesmaid Carry Seaward, did not speak. So that the cards had all to be shuffled again, and eventually she got four very pretty attendants to the altar. Barbara and her husband were away honeymooning; and she didn't like to ask Captain Lyster, having a perfect recollection of that morning in the library at Bissett, and thinking that his presence on such an occasion would probably render them both extremely uncomfortable.

But altogether the wedding went off with success; for the bishop was not only impressively solemn during the ceremony, but was pleasantly jocose afterwards, cracked tepid little jokes with infinite gusto; and a tepid jokelet from a bishop is worth more than a brilliant *mot* from a professional wit. And the company, though not very brilliant in intellect, was quite brilliant enough to laugh when a bishop said a good thing; and every body was very well dressed; and the wedding presents, duly set out on a side-table, made a splendid show. The Schröders were to the fore in the matter of wedding presents; the City magnates of the Townshend connexion did pretty well, so far as silver tea-services, and wine-coolers, and ice-pails, and fish knives and forks, and splendidly carved ivory tankards with massive silver covers, were concerned, and in all the usual wedding-gift non-

sense of butter-dish and card-bowl; but the Schröders gave diamond-necklaces and sets of turquoises
and opals in old-fashioned filigree settings, and
tiny watches from Leroy's, costing 3000 francs,
. and Barbedienne's rarest bronzes, and the choicest
carvings from the Frankfort Zeil. Mr. Schröder,
too, had taken his bride elect, two days before
the marriage, to Long Acre, and shown her the
neat little single brougham, and the elegant open
carriage; and then had driven on to Rice's, and
had had trotted out the fast trotters and the elegant steppers, which had been reserved for them.
And Alice Townshend thought of all these things
as she stood at the altar beside the elderly gentleman with the small eyes and the stubbly gray
hair; and the shudder which passed through her,
as she solemnly vowed to honour and obey him,
was a little mitigated by the recollection of his
wealth, and her consequent future position.

The honeymoon was spent partly at Brussels,
partly at Paris, and then the newly-married couple
came home to their house in Saxe Coburg Square.
Fifteen years ago, just before the first Great Exhi-

bition (*the* Great Exhibition! we who had *gelebt und geliebt* before '51 know how poor the other one was in comparison to it!), the tract of land whereon Saxe Coburg, Gotha, Coleraine, and Dilkington Squares, Adalbert Crescent, and Guelph Place now stand, was known as Grunter's Grounds, and was tenanted by an honest market-gardener, who found a very remunerative market in Covent Garden for his cabbage cultivation. But Hodder, the great builder, marked the army of luxury marching rapidly west; and knowing that quarters must be found for it, saw in Grunter's Grounds the exact place for the erection of those squares, crescents, terraces, and places, of which his architect, Palladio Hicks, had so elaborately shown the elevation on paper, but had erected so few. Mr. Hodder discovered that the nurseryman was in the last eighteen months of his lease, and that Grunter's Grounds belonged to a charity, the trustees of which were always quarreling among themselves. This was enough for Hodder; he soon wormed his way into the confidence of some of the trustees; and eventually succeeded in getting the renewal of the lease refused to the market-gardener, and the ground made over to him, on building lease, at a very cheap rate. Now do you wonder why Mrs. Hodder drives one of the most stylish equipages in the Park; or why, in her amateur theatricals, she manages to get hold of all that extraordinary histrionic genius, which, by an odd concurrence of events, always accompanies the possession of a clerkship in the Treasury? That was a splendid speculation for Mr. Hodder. There are thirty-six houses in Saxe Coburg Square, for instance; and each of them lets at 320*l.* a-year. They are all, as Mr. Thackeray said of the Pyramids, " very big," and very ugly; great gaunt stuccoed erections, bow-windowed, plate-glassed, and porticoed after the usual prevalent pattern, with a small square courtyard looking into a mews behind, and Mr. Swiveller's prospect, " a delightful view of—over the way," in front. But they let wonderfully; it is the thing to live in that quarter; and hangers-on to the selvage of fashion, clerks in public offices, who have married into aristocratic poor families, and such-

like, will be found bargaining for a ghastly little
hole in Adalbert Crescent or Guelph Place, when
they could get a capital roomy house at Highgate
or Hampstead, with a big garden, in which their
"young barbarians" could be "all at play" from
morning till night, for far less money. Mr. Schröder's house was furnished very expensively, and,
considering all had been left to the upholsterer, in
not bad taste. The dining-room was in light oak,
carved high-backed chairs in green morocco; a
large massive round-table in the centre, with half-
a-dozen swinging moderator-lamps over it; War-
dour Street Rubenses and apocryphal ancestors on
the walls. Behind this the library in dark oak,
splendid writing-table, quaint old carved Daven-
port desk from a Carmelite monastery; wonderful
collection of books, the result of the blending of
two library sales at Hodgson's,—one the gathering
of a bibliomaniacal *virtuoso*, the other of a sporting
nobleman,—and before-letter proofs, after Landseer. The drawing-rooms I should utterly fail in
endeavouring to describe, so content myself by
remarking that they were halls of dazzling light,

—allowed by their worst enemies, the critics, to be "delicious;" by their most captious, to be "effective,"—splendidly furnished, and opening on to conservatories and boudoirs and canvas-covered balconies.

Mr. Schröder was not the man to hide his candle under a bushel; nor, having spent a vast amount of money on his house and its decorations, to keep them solely for the contemplation of himself and his wife: so it was at his suggestion that the dinner-party and reception were organised. Mrs. Schröder at once gave her acquiescence; indeed, just at this period of her life she was in too dazed a state to do any thing more than follow suit. She knew her father to be wealthy, and always had lived in good style; but she also knew that her parent was a great tyrant—one of those "stern" persons so popular in novels; and she had had many visions of resisting him; of flying from his roof with some young lover not overburdened with riches; of love in a cottage, and other maniacal ideas of the same description; and now she found that the time had come and passed; that she had not resisted at all;

and that she was settled down with a gray-headed elderly husband, who was one of the richest men in London. It was not her childhood's dream, perhaps; but it was by no means uncomfortable; and Mrs. Schröder wisely determined to accept the riches, and to forget the grayness of the head; and went in for the dinner-party with spirit.

Husband and wife furnished about an equal complement of friends to the banquet, which was very splendid, but at first rather dull. Old Heinrich Schröder, who had not yet returned to Frankfort, was present; and as he spoke scarcely any English, he did not enliven the conversation; which, however, was often polyglot. The magnates from the City and their wives ate a good deal, and talked very little; while some of the younger and more aristocratic people brought in by Mrs. Schröder were silent as becomes "swells," and only occasionally worked eyebrow or shoulder telegraphs to each other, in silent wonder at, and depreciation of, their neighbours. Mr. Beresford began to be awfully bored, and tried topic after topic without meeting with the least success. At last, however, he seemed to have stumbled on one that awoke a certain amount of general interest.

"Seen your newly-elected brother-director of the Terra-del-Fuego Company yet, Mr. Schröder?" he asked.

"Colonel Levison?" said Mr. Schröder; "no, not yet; we've had no board-day since his election."

"Man of mark, sir," said an old gentleman, who had painted his chin and shirt-front with turtle-soup.

"What Levison is it, Beresford?" asked Captain Lyster, who was seated near Mrs. Schröder.

"Jack Levison; you know him. Wonderful life he's had!"

"Has he?" said Mrs. Schröder, on whom the dulness had settled like a pall. "Oh, do tell us about it, Mr. Beresford; that is, if you may."

"Oh, yes, I may," laughed Beresford; "though it's nothing much to tell. Jack was in the 9th, and came into five thousand pounds at his father's death; sold out; speculated in cotton, and made it twenty; speculated in hides, and lost every sixpence. Went out to Australia on the first discovery of gold; was a boot-black in Melbourne; actually had a stand and brushed boots, you know; afterwards was cad to the Ballarat omnibus; fact, give you my word! At last got up to the diggings; worked with varying luck, until at last turned up monster nugget, and hit upon a splendid vein; stuck to it quietly and made a fortune. Realised; came back to England, and has doubled it. Curious life, isn't it?"

" How very odd!" said Mrs. Schröder, trying to extract a remark from a very gorgeous lady on her right; " fancy, blacking boots!"

"And what do you call 'em to a 'bus?" said the lady, who though gorgeous was Clapham-born, and still possessed her native dialect.

" Must be clayver man," hazarded a tall thin gentleman, a light of the Draft and Docket Office, who was very short-sighted, and perpetually kept in his eye a glass, with which he endeavoured to focus somebody into conversation; hitherto hopelessly.

" Oh, yes," said his neighbour, a bald man

with cinnamon whiskers, whose life was passed in saying the wrong thing in the wrong place—"oh, yes; but don't you know he's Boswell Levison's brother. He's a Jew!"

Every body looked involuntarily at old Heinrich Schröder, about whose origin there could be no doubt, and who had that face which you may see repeated by hundreds in the Frankfort Juden-Gasse.

"Ha! ha!" said the old gentleman, catching the last word, and finding himself the centre of attraction; "was Chew! ya, zo; Chew ist goot."

Mr. Schröder turned a dull lead colour, and a general awe-struck silence fell upon the company, which was broken by Beresford, who, again coming to the rescue, said:

"You knew Levison, Monkhouse? We stayed together in his uncle's house two years ago."

The man with the eye-glass made a vain attempt to focus Beresford, and said, "Did we?"

"Yes, of course we did. You recollect, at Macarum's, near Elgin?"

Mr. Monkhouse dropped his glass from his eye

and looked up to the ceiling for inspiration; then, re-fixing it, said, " Oh, ah! Elgin! I know!—where the marble comes from?"

The Levison subject now being evidently exhausted, and the conversation becoming hopelessly idiotic, Captain Lyster strikes in at a tangent, and asks Mrs. Schröder whether she has seen any thing recently of her friend Mrs. Churchill,—Miss Lexden that was.

Mrs. Schröder replies in the negative, adding that she had called upon Barbara " in, oh, such a strange street!" but had not found her at home: the Churchills had been asked to dine there that day, but had declined on account of Mr. Churchill's engagements. It was, however, probable that they might come in the evening. Hearing the name of Churchill mentioned, Mr. Beresford chimes in.

" Ah, by the way, the Churchills! friends of yours, Mrs. Schröder! How are they getting on? Love-match, and all that kind of thing, hey? Clever man, Churchill; but should have kept to his own set; married the daughter of his printer or publisher, or some fellow of that sort; not taken away one of our stars."

"What do you mean by his own set, Mr. Beresford?" said Lyster, rousing himself. "Mr. Churchill, I take it, is a gentleman in every sense of the word. I don't know whom you have been accustomed to associate with, but I never saw a better-bred man."

Mr. Beresford pauses for a moment, startled at the attack: then a smile passes over his face as he says, "I didn't impugn your friend's breeding, Captain Lyster; but I suppose even such a Corydon as you would allow the folly of a love-match with no money on either side?"

It is probable that Captain Lyster might have replied, even seeing, clearly as he did, that the tendency of the conversation was towards an argument in which he would have to exert himself; but the cinnamon-whiskered man, who had been waiting for an opportunity of speaking, now saw his chance, and burst forth—"Love-match!" said he; "no money on either side! What, then? Do you imagine that two people, young, attached

to each other, who risk a—a—what d'ye call um?
—fight in the great battle of life"—looking round
and repeating " in the great battle of life—are
not much happier than those who make, what you
may call, sordid matches? Thus, for the sake of
argument, an elderly man marries a young girl;
nothing in common between them; she simply
married for position, or to oblige her parents;
and he—well, I think we know the contemptible
figure he cuts : a case of buying and selling, as
you would say in the City, eh, Schröder?" and
the cinnamon-coloured man, who was great at a
debating-society, looked in triumph at his host.

Mr. Schröder, more leaden-coloured than ever,
said, " Certainly." Mrs. Schröder, who had been
looking down at the table and playing with her
dessert-knife, rose with the rest of the ladies and
left the room. After their departure, the West-
end section, including Beresford, Lyster, and
Monkhouse, seemed to get silent and abstracted;
while Mr. Schröder's particular friends from the
City, the bank-directors and public-company men,
re-invigorated themselves with port, and discussed

the politics of Threadneedle Street and the chances
of change in the discount rate in hoarse whispers.
Solemn dulness fell upon the West-end division:
Lyster dropped into a semi-dose; Mr. Monkhouse
tried to focus the talkers one by one, but failing,
fell to polishing his eye-glass and admiring his
nails; the cinnamon-whiskered man cut into the
conversation once in the wrong place, and, having plainly showed himself to be an idiot, was
promptly extinguished; and Beresford fell into a
dreamy state, in which his liabilities ranged themselves in horrible array before him, and he went
into wild speculations as to how they might be
met. While in this state he became conscious of
old Mr. Townshend's voice, laying down the law,
in most imperative style, on matters of finance,
and suddenly he remembered his promise to Simnel. He waited for his opportunity when Mr.
Townshend ceased for an instant, and then said:
" My dear Mr. Schröder, you can't tell how horrible it is for us impecunious people to listen to
this tremendously ingotted talk. We look upon
you as a dozen Sindbad the Sailors, each having

found his own peculiar treasure in the Valley of Diamonds. Ah! if it were only given to me to fathom the secret of money-making!"

The City section were pleased at this concession, and took the remarks as complimentary. Mr. Schröder smiled, and said sententiously: "Business has its cares as well as its pleasures." Mr. Townshend nodded his head, saying, "You gentlemen despise our prosaic ways and business routine; with you—"

"Business routine!" exclaimed Beresford. "Why, you make a fortune by the arrival of a telegram, by the nod of a cabinet-minister's head. I'm not so ignorant of these mercantile matters as you may fancy. When I was in the habit of staying with my intimate friend Pigott, of the firm of Pigott and Wells—"

"What name did you say?" asked Mr. Townshend, with a blanched face.

"Pigott and Wells," repeated Beresford slowly, looking at him steadfastly; "merchants of Combcardingham. Do you know the firm?"

"No, not at all. That is—I—" and Mr.

Townshend's teeth chattered as he gulped down a bumper of port and cowered in his chair, as a tremendous knock, reverberating through the house, announced the arrival of the first guests for the reception.

The reception. *Item*, Herr Klavierspieler, the celebrated *pianiste*, who was so full of soul, and so mysterious, and so thin, and so long-haired, and so silent. All sorts of stories afloat about Herr Klavierspieler,—that he communed with spirits; that he was a ghoule; that he was consuming away under an unrequited passion for an Austrian countess of excessive haughtiness; whereas in real truth he was the son of a saddler in the Breite Strasse of Dresden, and his liver was deranged, perhaps by his eating five heavy meals a day, and, save when he was playing in public, never being without a pipe in his mouth. *Item*, M. Bloffski, the Pole, *the* violincellist of the world, a fat man in spectacles, who perspired a great deal, breathed through his nose, had a red-cotton pocket-handkerchief, and played his instrument

divinely.   *Item*, Mr. Schrink, musical critic of the *Statesman* newspaper, a little man with a humpback and a frightfully sensitive ear; a little man who would cower and shrink under false notes, and stamp and growl under bad singing; a little man whom every one hated, and who did not particularly like himself.   *Item*, Fräulein Wünster, one of those German young ladies who, ever since Jenny Lind's success, have been imported into England under the firm idea that they were " going to do it," and who, having filled up gaps in the Hanover Square and St. James's Hall concerts, have returned to *Vaterland* without having made the smallest mark.   Mr. Dabb, fashionable artist, whose portrait of Mr. Schröder decorated the walls, was there; as was Mr. Fleem, the author of *Fashion and Satire*—a young gentleman who, for a cynic, seemed on remarkably good terms with himself and his fellow-creatures. Mr. Pringle and Mr. Prescott arrived together; and just after the gentlemen came up from the dining-room, Mr. and Mrs. Churchill were announced.

If Mrs. Churchill had been the Empress of Austria or the Queen of the Cannibal Islands, she could not have entered the room more haughtily, or created a greater effect. She was dressed in a plain dark-gray silk, with a bunch of scarlet geraniums in her hair, and a black-lace shawl over her shoulders. Her little head was erect, her delicate nostrils distended, and her eye seemed to challenge any unpleasant remark. Frank Churchill was, as usual, quiet and sedate; but it was evident he marked the impression which his wife made, and was pleased thereby. Was he pleased with the expression of her face, as he marked it contracted for an instant, though immediately afterwards the features resumed their calm statuesque immobility? Was he pleased with the tone of her voice, which became a little hard and metallic, instead of that soft whispering which he knew as hers? Barbara's trial was on her at that instant: she had returned to that society in which she had all her life lived; those luxuries, which had been in daily use, were around her, after she had been for weeks absent from them; the mere size of the rooms, the light-

ing, the perfume, the presence of guests,—all
seemed to render the events of the past months
as a dream; and she had to bring her presence
of mind into play to argue with herself.

Mrs. Schröder rushed up to her at once; no
doubt of the *empressement* of her manner! affection
a little too palpable, as Barbara thought.

"Oh, Barbara darling! so glad you're come!
I thought you'd disappointed us. How late you
are!"

"Frank was detained; as I expected, Alice;
make him explain himself."

"No occasion for that, I hope, Mrs. Schröder,"
said Churchill; "the slaves of the lamp, you
know!"

"Oh, there! that horrible business! your constant excuse; you're all alike. Gustav! Gustav!
here's Mr. Churchill excusing himself from being
late, and pleads business; take him away, and
discuss the wretched subject together. I want to
talk to Barbara,—a long talk. No, Gustav! I don't
care what you say about my duties as hostess: I
will talk to my old friend!" So Schröder and

Churchill went off, and Alice and Barbara seated themselves in a far window.

"Now, Barbara dear, tell me every thing. I needn't ask you if you're happy; that's a matter of course. Do you like your house? Is the boudoir in pale-green silk, as we always said we'd have it? Mine's in rose-colour; but that's Gustav's taste; I always liked your notion best."

"My boudoir, Alice? you forget."

"Oh! so I do. How ridiculous! But look here, Barbara darling; you'll come out for a drive with me whenever I fetch you?"

"Oh, thanks, Alice; I'm too far out of your way to be fetched often."

"Not a bit, Barbara; what else have the horses to do? though it *is* a difficult place to find out. Edwards—the coachman, I mean—had never heard of it, though he knows all sorts of short cuts; and we had to ask our way perpetually."

Barbara had something on the tip of her tongue, but it was never framed into words. She contented herself with saying, "the situation is handy for my husband, you know. I should not like the thought that he had far to come late at night."

"Oh! is he ever out late at night? How dreadful! how dull you must be! how wretched for you! I should make my maid sit up and read me to sleep."

"There has been no need for any such violent measures at present," said Barbara, with a slight smile. "Frank has managed to do his work at home, hitherto; but of course there may be occasions when he will be obliged to be out."

"You must come to us then. Promise! won't you, Barbara dear? You'll like Mr. Schröder; at least I think you will. He's very quiet; but so kind-hearted and thoughtful. Oh, Captain Lyster! how you startled me!"

"Very sorry, Mrs. Schröder," drawled the Captain, creeping leisurely towards them; "wouldn't have put you out for the world; but this is scarcely fair, you know; two ladies monopolising each other when we're dying to talk to them; and we're left to listen to that horrible hirsute wretch who's thumping the piano."

" Klavierspieler a horrible wretch! Did you hear that, Barbara? Well, Captain Lyster, I won't monopolise Mrs. Churchill any more, and you shall have a chat with her;" and Mrs. Schröder walked off, laughing. Barbara had been looking at Mr. Schröder, who was standing in the doorway talking with Frank Churchill; and had noticed his face fall as Lyster approached them. When Mrs. Schröder moved away, her husband seemed relieved.

Captain Lyster sat down by Barbara, and talked long, and for him earnestly. She saw at once that he wanted to be numbered among her friends; and in a score of little delicate sentences he conveyed to her his appreciation of her conduct in marrying a man whom she loved, in spite of the opposition of her friends, his respect for her husband's character and talents, and his desire to serve them. Then he turned the conversation upon Mrs. Schröder; and Barbara noticed that his manner changed; that he hesitated, and kept his eyes down, as he wondered whether she were happy; whether she loved her husband; whether it had really been her duty to obey her father's will, and not consult her own inclinations, as people said had been the case. For the first time a light broke upon Barbara, and she knew Captain Lyster's story as plainly as if he had told it to her in so many words. Following his glance as he stopped speaking, she saw that it rested on Alice Schröder, to whom Mr. Beresford was now talking, bending over her chair with great apparent devotion; and looking from them to Mr. Schröder, Barbara remarked that the gloom had returned to his face, while Frank Churchill himself looked somewhat annoyed.

It was not without a very great deal of trouble that Mr. Pringle had induced his friend Prescott to accompany him to Saxe Coburg Square. Even after that gentleman had given a reluctant consent he withdrew it, and on the very morning of the reception Mr. Pringle was not aware whether or not he should have to go alone. For Mr. Prescott was very much in love with Kate Mellon still: that interview in the Park had by no means had the effect of curing him of his passion;

although, being a sensible young fellow, he saw that there was not the slightest use in giving way to it.

"He's a thoroughly changed buffer, is Jim, sir!" Mr. Pringle would remark of him; "he used to be the cheeriest of birds; always good for going out some where, and no end of fun; always in tip-top spirits, and the best chap out. But now he sits in his chambers, and smokes his pipe, and grizzles himself to death, pretty near; wishing he'd got more money, and all sorts of things. That won't do, you know! He must be picked up and trotted out; and the man for that line of business is yours truly." In pursuance of which determination Mr. Pringle opened a system of attack on his friend, and in the first place insisted that they should go together to Mr. Schröder's reception. Even at the last, when Prescott gave in his final consent, it was under strong protest. "I shall be dreary, old boy; and you'll be sorry you took me. You know I'm not very good company just now, George. I've not got over—"

"All right; I know. 'Tell me, my heart,

can this be?' &c. But we'll have some dinner at Simpson's, and a bottle of old port; and that'll set you up, and make you see life under a different aspect, as they say in novels."

The dinner was very good; and finding his friend still silent and low-spirited, Mr. Pringle exerted himself to rouse him. He was very well known at the dining-rooms, and called the waiters by their Christian names, and asked after their families, and little events in their private lives.

Mr. Prescott could not help laughing at the absurdities perpetrated by his friend, and gradually his spirits revived. After dinner they went to Mr. Pringle's chambers, and smoked and had some hot whisky-and-water, which, coming after the port-wine, had a very hilarious effect upon Mr. Pringle, who then wanted to "go out some where," and not to go to the Schröders at all; but Mr. Prescott overruling this, they dressed and went. Mr. Pringle—and especially Mr. Pringle after half a bottle of port-wine and a couple of tumblers of whisky-punch—was a trying person to go about with, and Prescott had to call him to order several times. When they arrived at the house, and were asked their names, he gave them as the Duke of Wellington and Mr. Babbage; and on the servant's being about gravely to repeat them, he stopped him, saying they did not wish their names announced, as they were detectives come on very private business. On the staircase he feigned a wild terror at the powdered heads of the footmen; asked "how they came so white;" by nature or not? and altogether so behaved himself that Mr. Prescott declared he would not enter the room with him.

Once in the room, Mr. Pringle toned down visibly, and conducted himself like an ordinary mortal. He was very friendly with Alice Schröder, and expressed poignant regret at Mr. Townshend's sudden indisposition (for that worthy gentleman declined to come upstairs after dinner; Beresford's mention of Pigott and Wells had been too much for him), though secretly Mr. Pringle was pleased at missing his godfather, whom he was accustomed to regard as the essence of sternness; and he was introduced to Churchill, of whom he spoke the next day at the office as a "deuced clever fellow, a literary bird;" and he listened for a few minutes to Klavierspieler's pianoforte-fireworks ; and then went down and got some refreshment. He endeavoured to induce Mr. Prescott to accompany him ; but that gentleman not merely absolutely declined, but addressed his friend in strong words of warning, and declared that as for himself he was thoroughly happy where he was.

Indeed, once more in society, surrounded by well-looking, well-dressed people, listening to music and conversation in a splendidly-appointed house, Mr. Prescott began to think to himself that the solitary pipe-smokings in dreary chambers, the shutting himself away from the world, and giving himself up to melancholy, was rather a mistake. Of course the grand cause of it all remained unaltered,—he never could get over his passion, he never would give up thinking of Kate,—and just then he started as he heard a light, musical, girlish voice behind him say, " It *is* James Prescott!" He turned rapidly round, and saw two or three people standing by him; one of whom, a very pretty fresh-coloured buxom girl, stepped forward, laughed as he made a rather distant bow, and said, "You don't recollect me! Oh, what a horridly bad compliment!"

"It is excessively absurd, to be sure, on my part, I know. I cannot, by Jove! Emily Murray!" Prescott burst out as the face recurred to his memory.

"Emily Murray, of course!" said the young lady, still laughing; "Why, what ages since we've met! not since you left Havering; and how's the dear Vicar and the girls? which of them are married? I should so like to see them; and you—you're in some Government Office we heard; which is it? and—"

"I must come to Mr. Prescott's rescue, Emily, if you'll introduce me. You've stunned him with questions," said an elderly lady standing by.

"Oh, aunt, how can you say so! James— Mr. Prescott,—I don't know which I ought to say; but I always used to say James,—this is my aunt, Mrs. Wilmslow, with whom we're staying. I say we, for papa is in town; but his gout was threatening; so he wouldn't come to-night."

" My brother will be very pleased to see you, though, Mr. Prescott," said Mrs. Wilmslow; " I know he has the kindliest recollection of your father at Havering. Will you come and lunch with us to-morrow?"

Mr. Prescott accepted with thanks, and Mrs. Wilmslow moved back to her party; but Emily Murray stayed behind, and they had a very long conversation; during which he settled not merely that he would lunch in Portland Place on the next day, but that he would afterwards accompany Miss Murray and some of her friends in their subsequent ride. As Miss Murray departed with her friends, Mr. Pringle came up and apologised for having left his friend so much alone. " Very sorry, old fellow, but I got into an argument with an old German buffer downstairs. Very good fellow, but spoke very shy English. Told me he was nearly eighty years old; and that he accounted for his good health by having been always in the habit of taking a walk past dinner. Took me full ten minutes to find out he meant *after* dinner. But I say, old fellow, I'm really sorry; you must have had a very slow evening."

"On the contrary," said Mr. Prescott, "I've enjoyed myself amazingly."

Mr. Pringle looked hard at his friend, and whistled plaintively.

CHAPTER III.

THE OLD OR THE NEW?

THIRTY years before the date of my story, Braxton Murray and Alan Prescott were college friends. Braxton was a gentleman commoner of Christchurch; Alan, a scholar of Wadham. Braxton had four hundred a-year allowance from his father, and the direct succession to one of the richest estates in Kent. Alan had his scholarship, seventy pounds a-year exhibition from a country foundation-school, and another fifty allowed him by his uncle. The disparity between the positions of the two young men was vast, but they were thoroughly attached to each other; and when Braxton had succeeded his father, and the old vicar of Havering died, Braxton Murray sent for Alan Prescott, then doing duty as a curate and usher in a suburban school, and presented

him with the vicarage of Havering. That was
a happy time in both their lives; the income of
the Vicar was small, certainly, but so was the
parish, and the duties were light; and having
only himself, his wife, and a son and daughter
to provide for, and being constantly in the receipt of presents from his friend and patron,
the Rev. Alan Prescott did very well indeed.
Situate in the heart of Kent, no prettier spot
than Havering can be found; and Brooklands,
the squire's place, is the gem of the county. In
the bay-window of the old dining-room, over-
hanging the fertile valley through which the
Medway lies like a thread of silver, the two
men would sit drinking their claret, discussing
old university chums or topics of the day, and
pausing occasionally to look at the gambols of
the Vicar's son, Jim, and the Squire's only
daughter, Emily, who were the merriest of little
lovers. But as years went by and the Vicar's
family steadily increased,—first by twin girls,
then by a bouncing boy, and finally by a little
crippled girl,—and as, each year, expenses grew

heavier, Alan Prescott was somewhat put to it to obtain the necessary connexion of those two ends, the means of bringing which together puzzles so many of us all our lives; and when the governors of the foundation-school where he had been usher, remembering his abilities, wrote to offer him the vacant head-mastership, he was too poor to refuse it. Duffborough, a big, staring, gaunt manufacturing town, perched on one of the bleakest of the northern hills, was a bad exchange for beaming little Havering, with its smiling orchards and glorious hop-gardens; and the society of the purse-proud, cold, stuck-up calico-men was heartbreaking after the ease and warmth of Braxton Murray's companionship. But Alan Prescott felt the spurs of need, and buckled to his work like a man. An active correspondence was kept up between him and the Squire of Havering; and occasionally,—once in the course of four or five years, perhaps,—he had spent a week at Brooklands; but it was too expensive to remove his family; and consequently, until that evening in Saxe Coburg Square, James

Prescott had not seen Emily Murray since they were children together, playing out in the old dining-room at Brooklands.

Emily Murray had been a pretty child; had become a beautiful girl. There was no doubt about her; one look into those honest brown eyes would have convinced you that she was thorough. A plump rosy-rounded bud of woman; a thoroughly English girl, void of affectation, conceit, and trickery; clean, clear, honest, wholesome, and loving. As she talked to James Prescott of the old days at Havering, she spoke out freely, referring to bygone gambols and fun with frank laughter and many a humorous reminiscence; and when she suggested his joining their riding-party the next day, she looked him straight in the face without the smallest shadow of entanglement or guile. To her own brother her manner had not been different, Prescott thought, as, after they had parted, he recalled every word, every glance; and he wished for a moment that there had been something different in it, a trifle more tenderness, a hand-pressure, a sly upward glance, or—and then he flung such nonsense behind him, and was delighted to remember the warmth of her recognition, the cheeriness of her chat. She was nothing to him, of course; his doom was fixed; he had loved, and—and yet how pretty she was! how perfectly gloved! how charmingly dressed! what a pleasure it was to feel that you were talking to a lady! to know that no slanginess would offend the eye, no questionable *argot* grate upon the ear; to feel that—and then Mr. Prescott remembered how the idol of his soul had called him "Jim," ay, and "old buffer;" how she had smoked cigars, and used maledictions towards refractory animals; how there had been all kinds of odd discussions about all kinds of odd people before her; and how he had seen men take wine without stint, and smoke cigars in her face, and wear their hats before her, without the smallest self-restraint. And, smoking a final pipe before turning into bed, Mr. Prescott pondered on these things long and earnestly.

Mr. Prescott found a warm welcome awaiting him. Mrs. Wilmslow had been impressed with his manners and appearance, and old Mr. Murray had a yearning for the friend of his youth, and longed to receive that friend's son with open arms. A hale pleasant gentleman, Mr. Murray, with that wonderful cleanliness which is never seen out of England, with polished bald head fringed with iron-gray hair, ruddy complexion, keen little blue eyes, and brilliant teeth. He wore a slipper on his right foot, but hobbled forward, nevertheless, and gave the young man a hearty shake of the hand.

"Glad to see you, Jim! Little Jim you were; but, by Jove! I should not like to carry you on my back now, as I have done many a time. Very glad to see you! Old times come again, by George! Trace every feature of your face, and can almost see Magdalen tower behind your back—you're so like your father. How's the Vicar, eh? I'll drag him out of that infernal spinning-jenny place yet, and give him a breather across the home-copse at Havering before next season's over."

Prescott said that his father was well and jolly, but scarcely up to shooting now, he had had so little practice lately.

"So much the more reason we should give it him, then! He used to be a crack shot; one of the few men I've seen shoot a brace of woodcock right and left! And walk! by George, he'd walk me into—has he had any gout?"

"Not yet, sir;—a threatening last year."

"Bravo!" roared the old gentleman; "I've got some 20-port that shall bring that threatening to real effect, if he'll only drink enough of it. And to think that Pussy should have found you out!"

"Pussy?" said Mr. Prescott.

"Emily, of course! a wayward gentle puss who never shows her claws!" and at that moment Emily entered the room, and advanced towards Prescott with frank smile and outstretched hand.

Luncheon passed off pleasantly enough. The old gentleman rattled on incessantly, and availed himself of Prescott's presence, and Mrs. Wilmslow's distracted attention consequent thereupon, to take three bumpers of dry sherry, instead of that one half-glass to which, by doctor's orders, he was so strictly relegated. Mrs. Wilmslow was thoroughly charmed with Prescott, led him on to talk of his home-life, of his office friends, and seemed to regard him, with real interest. Emily was less talkative than she had been the previous evening, and seldom looked up from the table; but she joined readily in the conversation, and none were too pleased when the horses were announced.

"Got a horse, Jim?" asked the Squire. "That's right! hope it'll carry you all right, though one never knows any thing about these hired hacks. You might have ridden the cob, if I'd known you'd been coming earlier! This is his third day's rest, and the cob will be about as fresh as paint when I get across him again. Not that I care much for your Rotten-Row riding—dull work that, up and down, up and down! The Vicar and I—we used to go to work in a little more business-like fashion than that! I suppose he never gets a day's run now? Ah! thought not! Those spinning-jenny locals would think it unprofessional for a parson to follow hounds, eh? There, bless you pussy! good-by, child! and good-by to you, young Jim! Call here again in a day or two, and we'll settle about your coming to Havering in the vacation—and the Vicar too, d'ye hear?"

"I'm getting rather nervous about my responsibility, Miss Murray," said Prescott, as they passed through into the hall. "I don't think I've forgotten my old knack of mounting. You needn't fear my not lifting you high enough, or jerking you over the side, I mean; but I've never seen your amazonship yet, and if any thing should happen—"

"Oh, don't fear that, James—Mr. Prescott, I mean!" said Emily with a clear ringing laugh. "You'll mount me rightly enough, I know: and as for looking after me afterwards, I forgot to tell you my riding-mistress would be with us."

"Your riding-mistress!" but as he spoke, the footman threw open the street-door; and the first thing that met his glance was a well-known figure sitting erect on a black thorough-bred. Kate Mellon! no one else. James Prescott had watched too often the rounded outline of that compact figure, the fall of that dark-blue skirt, the *pose* of that neat little chimney-pot hat, under which the gold-shot

hair was massed in a clump behind, not to recognise them all at the first glance. Kate Mellon, by
all that was marvellous! Two young ladies, also
mounted, were with her; and a groom was leading
another horse, with a side-saddle on it for Emily
Murray, and another groom was leading the very
presentable hack which Prescott had engaged from
Allen's. As she caught sight of Prescott, Kate
gave one little scarcely-perceptible start, and then
saluted Miss Murray with uplifted whip. Prescott
swung Emily to her saddle, and the cavalcade
started.

"You see I have brought a cavalier, Miss
Mellon," said Emily, with a smile; "though I don't
know whether such an encumbrance is permissible;
but this is Mr. Prescott, whom I have known for
a very long time. James, this is Miss Mellon,
who is good enough to superintend my clumsiness
on horseback, and who is the very star of horse-
women herself."

Kate started a little at the "James," but
merely repeated the whip salutation, and said,
"Mr. Prescott and I have met before, Miss

Murray. Besides, you're coming it too strong about yourself! you're quite able to take care of yourself now, and have no clumsiness left, whatever you might have had at first. This has relieved me of some of my charge; for these two young ladies will want all my eyes, and another to spare, if I had it. Perhaps you'll not mind my riding forward with them, and you and Mr. Prescott can follow us; you're both of you to be trusted —with your horses, I mean!" and she smiled shortly, and cantering on, joined the anonymous young ladies in front.

You see it is perfectly right to tell a man who is desperately smitten with you that he is on the wrong tack; that though you have a great regard for him as a friend, you cannot reciprocate his love-passion; and that the whole affair is ill-judged, and should properly be put a stop to at once. But when you come upon him suddenly, within three weeks, evidently consoling himself by dangling at the heels of another woman—well, there is something provoking in it, to say the least! Kate Mellon was thoroughly honest during all that last interview with Prescott in Rotten Row, but she scarcely expected *this*.

So they rode on in two divisions; and the young ladies in front, who were the daughters of a picture-dealer who had recently risen from nothing, and who were in the greatest state of fright at the unaccustomed exercise, were surprised to find a tone of asperity at first tinging their mistress's instructions at being told of their rounded shoulders and their heavy hands, in far plainer terms than had been hitherto employed. But this severity gradually subsided as they went on; and as Kate thought to herself how all was for the best, and how, instead of being annoyed, she ought to do every thing she could to help the fortunes of one who had been so stanchly gallant to her, until he was repulsed. As for the couple behind, they got on splendidly; Emily looked to the greatest advantage on horseback; and Prescott could scarcely take his eyes from her as he watched the graceful manner in which she sat her horse, and as he listened to the encomiastic remarks which her appearance extracted from the passers-by. He talked to her of the old days, and she answered without an ounce of coquetry or affectation; and she spoke of her father, of her happiness in her home, of the little simple duties and pleasures in their village, and of other little such-like matters, in an honest way that touched James Prescott deeply, and sent purer, calmer thoughts into his heart than had found lodging there for many months.

After a couple of hours in the Row the party returned to Mrs. Wilmslow's, where Emily bade them farewell, and Prescott also alighted, giving up his horse to the groom waiting for it. Kate Mellon saw her other pupils to their home close by, and then turned into the Row again, intending to have one final gallop on her way to the Den. She was at full speed when she heard the dull thud of a horse's hoofs close behind her, and turning saw Mr. Simnel. In a minute he was by her side.

"How d'ye do, Kate?" said he, reining-in his big hunter; "I came on the chance of seeing you here."

"How do, Simnel?" said Miss Mellon, shortly, "what do you want?"

"I want you to say when I can come up to the Den and have half-an-hour's chat with you, Kate."

"And I tell you, never! as I've told you before. Look here, Simnel," said she, pulling up short; "let's have this out now. I don't like you; I never did, and I never shall! and I don't want you at my place. Do you understand?"

"Perfectly," said Simnel, with a hard smile; "and yet I think I must come. I want to say something specially particular to you."

"What about? What you've said before? About yourself?"

"No," said Simnel, smiling as before; "I never say things twice over. I want to talk to you about a friend of ours — Charles Beresford."

"Charles Beresford?—what of him?"

"That's just what I propose to come and tell you."

Their eyes met. The next instant Kate cast hers down as she said, "I shall be at home on Friday from two till six. You can come then."

"You may depend on me," said Simnel; "I'll not bore you any longer." He raised his hat with perfect politeness, turned his horse, and rode slowly away.

CHAPTER IV.

THREE months' experience sufficiently indoctri
nated Barbara Churchill into her new life. At
the end of that time she could scarcely have been
recognised as the Barbara Lexden who had held
her own for three seasons, and done undisputed
havoc among the detrimentals: not that she was
changed in appearance; that grand *hauteur*, that
indefinable something of delicacy, breeding, and
refinement, was even more noticeable than ever
if any thing her nostrils were more frequently expanded, her lips more constant in their
curve; nor had her eyes lost their brightness,
her figure its trim form, her walk its grace and
elegance. Though Parker had long since served

under another mistress, Barbara's hair had never been more artistically arranged than by her own hands; and though her dress had been modified from the nearest approach to excess in the prevailing fashion which good taste would permit to the merest simplicity, she had never, even in the height of her queendom, been more becomingly attired than in the plain silk dresses and simple linen collars and cuffs which she donned in Great Adullam Street. Where was the change, then? whence the source of the alteration? In truth she herself could scarcely tell; or if the idea ever rose in her mind she thrust it out instantly, arguing within herself, in a thousand unimpressive, undecisive, unsatisfactory ways, that she did *not* feel as she had imagined, and that she was merely "a little low."

That phrase was Frank Churchill's bane. He would return from the *Statesman* office, where, after the regular daily consultation, he had remained and written his leader (Harding always hitherto had managed to free his friend from night-work), and would find his wife with red-rimmed eyelids and the final traces of a past shower. At first he was frightened at these manifestations, would tenderly caress her, and ask her what had happened. Nothing! always nothing! no cross, no domestic anxiety, no special trouble. But then something must have happened. Frank's logical spirit, long trained, refused to accept an effect without a cause; and at length, after repeated questioning, he would learn from Barbara that she was "a little low" that day. A little low! What on earth had she had to be a little low about? And then Frank would imagine that there were more things in women than were dreamt of in his philosophy; and would pet her and coax her during dinner, and restore her somewhat to herself, until he took up his review or his heavy reading, when the "little low" fit would come on again; and after half an hour's contemplation of the coals Barbara would burst into sobs and retire to bed. And then Frank, laying down his book and pondering over his final pipe, would first begin to think that he was badly treated; to review his conduct, and see whether any act of his during the day could have caused the "little lowness;" to imagine that Barbara was making mountains of molehills, and was losing that spirit which had been one great attraction to him; then gradually he would soften, would take into consideration the changes in the circumstances of her life; would begin to accuse himself of neglecting her, and preferring his reading at a time when she had a fair claim on his attention; and would finally rush off to implore her forgiveness, and pet her more than ever.

An infatuated fellow, this Frank Churchill; so happy in the possession of his wife, in the knowledge that she was his own, all his own, that nothing, not even the fact that she was occasionally a "little low," had power to damp his happiness for more than a very few minutes. He would sit at dinner, of an evening when she was engaged with her work and he had a book in front of him, in company when he could steal a minute from the general conversation, looking at her in rapt admiration; not one point of her beauty was lost upon him; the shape of her head; its *pose* on her neck; her delicate hands with that pink shell-like palm; those long tapering fingers and filbert nails; her rounded bust and slim waist,—all her special excellences impressed him more now than they had when he had first seen her; but, above all, he revelled in her "bred" appearance, in that indefinable something which seemed to lift her completely out of the set of people with which he saw her surrounded, and to show her by right the denizen of another sphere. If you could have persuaded Frank Churchill that another man held such opinions as these; that another man had such feelings with regard to his wife; and that through holding them he was induced to regard somewhat intolerantly those among whom he had hitherto moved, and from whom he had received the greatest kindness and friendship,—what words would have been scathing enough to have expressed Frank Churchill's disgust!

Yet such was undoubtedly the case. Churchill's most intimate friend was George Harding, —a man whom he reverenced and looked up to, but whom he, since his marriage, had often found himself pitying from the bottom of his soul. Not on his own account: loyal to his craft and steadfast in his friendship, Churchill thought there were few more desirable positions than the editorship of the *Statesman*, when as free from influence or partisanship as when Harding held the berth. It was because his friend was Mrs. Harding's husband that Churchill pitied him; though, indeed, Mrs. Harding was a very fair average kind of woman. A dowdy little person, Mrs. Harding; the daughter of a snuffy Welsh rector, who had written a treatise on "Aorists," and with whom Harding had read one long vacation,—a round-faced old-maidish little woman, classically brought up, who could construe Cicero fluently, and looked upon Horace (Q. Flaccus, I mean) as rather a loose personage. In the solitude of Plas-y-dwdllem, George Harding was thrown into the society of this young female. He did not fall in love with her—they were neither of them capable of any thing violent of that nature; but—I am reduced to the phraseology of the servants' hall to express my meaning—they "kept company together;" and when George took his degree and started in life as leader-writer for the *Morning Cracker* (long since defunct), he thought the best thing he could do for his comfort was to go for a run to Wales and bring back Sophia Evans as his wife. This he did; and they had lived thoroughly happily ever since. Mrs. Harding believed intensely in the *Statesman;* read it every day, from the title to the printer's name; knew the name of every contributor, and could tell who had done what at a glance. Her great pride in going out was to take one of the cards sent to the office, and observe the effect it made upon the receiving attendant at operas, flower-shows, or conversazioni. She always took care that the tickets for these last were sent to her; and her head-dress of black-velvet bows with pearl-beads hanging down behind was well to the fore whenever a mummy was unrolled, the fossil jawbone of an antediluvian animal was descanted on, or some sallow missionary presented himself at Burlington House, to be congratulated by hundreds of dreary people

on having escaped uneaten from some place to
which he never ought to have gone. She herself
was fond of having occasionally what she called
"a social evening." This recreation was held on
a Saturday, when there was no work at the *Statesman* office,. when the principal members of the
staff would be bidden, and when the condiments
provided would be brown-bread and butter rolled
into *cornets*, tea and coffee and lemonade, while the
recreation consisted in conversation (amongst men
who had met for every night during the past
twelve months), and in examining photographs
of the city of Prague. The ribald young men at
the office spoke of Mrs. Harding as " Plutarch,"
a name given to her one night when Mr. Slater,
the dramatic critic, asked her what novel she was
then reading, and she replied, " Novel, sir! Plutarch's Lives!" But they all liked her, notwith-
standing; and for her sake and their dear old
chief's did penitential duty at the occasional " social evenings" in Decorum Street.

Of course this little body had nothing in common with Mrs. Frank Churchill, and neither un-

derstood the other. George Harding had been so anxious that his wife should pay all honour to his friend's bride, that Mrs. Harding's was the first visit Barbara received. They did not study the laws of etiquette in Mesopotamia, or Mrs. Harding thought she would break the ice of ceremony with a friendly call; so she arrived one morning at 11 A.M. dressed for the occasion, and having sent up her card, awaited Barbara's advent in the drawing-room. No sooner had the servant shut the door and Mrs. Harding found herself alone than she minutely examined the furniture, saw where new things had replaced others with which she had been acquainted, mentally appraised the new car-pet, and took stock generally. The result was not satisfactory; an anti-macassar which Barbara had been braiding lay on the table, with the needle still in it. Mrs. Harding took it up between her finger and thumb, gazed at it contemptuously, and pro-nounced it "fal-lal;" she peeped into the leaves of a book lying open on the sofa, and shut them up with a sigh of "Novels! ah!" she turned over the music lying on the little cottage-piano which Frank

had hired for his wife, and again shrugged her
shoulders with an exclamation of distaste. Then
she sat herself down on a low chair with her back
to the light (an old campaigner, Mrs. Harding,
and seldom to be taken at a disadvantage), pulled
out and smoothed her dress all round her, settled
her ribbons, made a further incursion into the
territories of a refractory thumb in her cowskin
puce-coloured glove, which had hitherto refused
submission to the invader, and awaited the coming
of her hostess.

She had not long to wait. Frank had gone
out on business ; but he had so often spoken of
Harding as his dear friend, that Barbara, though
by no means gushing by nature,—indeed, if truth
must be told, somewhat proud and reserved,—had
made up her mind to be specially friendly to Mrs.
Harding; so she came sailing into the room with
outstretched hand and a smile on her face. Mrs.
Harding gave one glance at the full flowing figure,
the rustling skirts, and the outstretched hand ; she
acknowledged the superior presence, and then suddenly maxims learned in her youth in the still

seclusion of Plas-y-dwdllcm rose in her mind,—
maxims which inculcated a severe and uncompro-
mising deportment as the very acme of good breeding. So, instead of coming forward to meet Barbara
and responding to her apparent warmth, the little
woman stood up for a quarter of a minute, crossed
her hands before her, bowed, and sank into her
seat again. For an instant Barbara stopped, and
flushed to the roots of her hair; then, quickly perceiving it was merely ignorance which had caused
this strange proceeding on Mrs. Harding's part,
she advanced and seated herself near her visitor.

" You are a stranger in this neighbourhood?"
commenced Mrs. Harding.

Barbara, feeling that the admission would be
what policemen call " used against her," answered
in the affirmative.

" It's very healthy," said Mrs. Harding.

Barbara again assented.

" Do you like it?" asked Mrs. Harding.

" I can scarcely say. I have had so little opportunity of judging. It is very convenient for
where my husband has to go, and all that; but it

is a long way from that part of London which I know."

Two or three things in this innocently-intended speech jarred dreadfully on Mrs. Harding's feelings. That worthy matron had all the blood of Ap-somebody, a tremendously consonanted personage of Plas-y-dwdllem in old times, and she was irritable in the highest degree. But she made a great gulp at her rage, and only said, " Oh, you mean the *Statesman* Office ; yes, of course I ought to know where that is, considering Mr. Harding's position there ! We think this a very nice situation ; but, of course, when you've been brought up in Grosvenor Square, it's different ! What does Vokins charge you ?"

" I—I beg your pardon !" said Barbara. " Vokins ?"

" Yes ; Vokins the butcher !" repeated the energetic little woman. " Sevenpence or sevenpence-halfpenny for legs ? Your mother-in-law was the only woman in the neighbourhood who got 'em for sevenpence, and I'm most anxious to know whether he hasn't raised it since you came here."

" I'm sorry I'm unable to answer you," said Barbara ; " but hitherto my husband has paid the tradesmen's bills. " I've no doubt," she added, with a half-sneer, " that it shows great short-comings on my part; but it is the fact. I have hopes that I shall improve as I go on."

" Oh, no doubt," said Mrs. Harding, faintly. " Live and learn, you know." But she gave up Barbara Churchill from that time out. She, who had known the price of every article of domestic consumption since she was fourteen years old, and had fought innumerable hand-to-hand combats with extortionate tradesmen, looked upon this *insouciance* of Barbara's as any thing but a venial crime. A few other topics were started, feebly entered into, and dropped; and then Mrs. Harding took her leave, with faintly-expressed hopes of seeing her new-made acquaintance soon again.

That afternoon George Harding, returning home to dinner, was told by his wife that she had called on Mrs. Churchill.

" Ay !" said the honest old boy; " and what

did you make of her, Sophy? I'd trust your judgment in a thousand; and Frank has a high opinion of it, I know. Is she pretty, and clever, and managing, and all the rest of it?"

"Well, as to prettiness, George, she's not one of my style of beauties," said Mrs. Harding. "She's a tall slip of a woman, with straight features, such as you see on the old coins; and she's very stand-offish in her manners; and, as to managing—well, she's too fine a lady to know her tradespeople's names, or what she pays them."

George Harding whistled softly, and then plunged into his hashed mutton. He made but one remark, but that he repeated twice. "I told him to beware of swells. God knows I warned him. I told him to beware of swells."

That same night Mrs. Churchill told her husband of the visit she had had.

"I'm so glad!" said Frank. "I knew old George would send his wife first. Well, what do you think of Mrs. Harding, Barbara?"

"Oh, I've no doubt she meant every thing kindly, Frank," said Barbara. "She's—she's a right-meaning kind of woman, Frank, no doubt; but she's—she's not my style, you know."

Frank was dashed. "I don't exactly understand, dear. She was perfectly friendly?"

"Oh, perfectly! But she asked me all sorts of curious questions about the tradespeople, and the housekeeping, and that. So strange, you know."

"I confess I don't see any thing strange so far. She offered you the benefit of her experience, did she? Well, that was kind; and what was wanted, I think."

"Oh, I'm sorry you think it was wanted," said Barbara. "I didn't think any thing had gone wrong in the house."

"No, my darling, of course not," said Frank; "nothing—all is quite right. But, you know, housekeeping is Mrs. Harding's strong point; and young beginners like ourselves might learn from her with advantage. I think we must lay ourselves out for instruction in several matters, Barbara darling, from such persons as Mrs. Harding and my mother."

And Barbara said, "Oh, yes, of course." And

Frank did not notice that her little shoulders went up, and the corners of her little mouth went down, and her eyes sparkled in a manner which did not promise much docility on the part of one of the pupils thus to be instructed.

It took but a very short time for Barbara to discover that she and her mother-in-law were not likely to be the very best friends. On their first meeting the old lady was very much overcome, and welcomed her new daughter-in-law in all fulness of heart. And perhaps—though Barbara never knew it—it was at this first meeting that a feeling of disappointment was engendered in Mrs. Churchill's heart. For long brooding over the forthcoming events of that day, ere the new-married couple had returned to town, Mrs. Churchill had settled in her own mind that there were to be no jealousies between her and the new importation into the small family circle as to the possession of Frank, and that to that end the right plan would be to receive Barbara as her daughter, and to make her part recipient of that affection

which had hitherto only been lavished on Frank.
This idea she forthwith carried into execution,
kissing Barbara with great warmth, and addressing her as her dear child.   Unimpulsive Barbara,
though really pleased at her reception, accepted
the caresses with becoming dignity, offered her
cheek for the old lady's warm salute, and addressed her mother-in-law in tones which, though
by no means lacking in reverence, certainly had
no superfluity of love.   The old lady noticed it,
and ascribed it to timidity, or the natural shyness
of a young girl in a strange position ; she noticed
specially that Barbara invariably spoke to and of
her as " Mrs. Churchill ;" and before they parted
she said :

" My dear, you surely don't always intend to
speak to me in that formal manner.   I am your
mother now, Barbara ; won't you call me so ?"

" No, dear Mrs. Churchill—no, if you please !
I have never called any one by that name since
I lost my own mother, and—and I cannot do so,
indeed."

Mrs. Churchill simply said, " Very well, my

dear." But in what afterwards became a gaping wound, this may be looked upon as the first abrasion of the skin. That gave the old lady a notion that her daughter-in-law's tactics were to be purely defensive, that there was to be no compromise, and that she, the old lady, was clearly to understand that her position was on the other side of the gabions and the fascines, the stone walls and the broad moat; that by no means was the key of the citadel to be considered as in her possession.

When relations of this kind in one family begin to be *à tort et à travers*, there is no end to the horrible complications arising out of them. Mrs. Churchill attempted to initiate Barbara into the mysteries of housekeeping, and the art of successfully combating nefarious tradesmen; but the success which attended the old lady's efforts may be guessed from Barbara's interview with Mrs. Harding. She tried to get Barbara to walk out with her; but Barbara had not been accustomed to walk in London streets, and was timid at crossings,—which made the old lady irate; and was frightened at the way in which men stared, and on some occasions spoke out unreservedly their opinions of her beauty. She had liked the outspoken admiration of the crowd, as she sat well forward in the carriage on drawing-room days; but then she knew that she had Jeames with his long cane in reserve in case of need; though I doubt whether Jeames would have been more useful in case of actual attack than old Mrs. Churchill, who invariably resented these unsolicited compliments to her daughter-in-law with a snort of defiance, and who usually carried a stout umbrella with a ferule at the end, which would have made a very awkward weapon, and which she would have wielded with right good will. Misunderstandings were constant: after the first few occasions of their meeting, Barbara did not ask Mrs. Churchill to the house for fear of appearing formal; whereupon the old lady, when Frank called at her lodgings, asked what she had done to be exiled from her son's house. Pacified and settled as to this point, the old lady, to show her forgiveness, called in so frequently, that Barbara told her husband she knew her housekeeping was not perfection; but that she had not expected a system of *espionnage,* which was evidently kept on her by his mother. When Mrs. Churchill dined at their house, Barbara, for fear of appearing extravagant, would have a very simple joint and pudding; whereupon the old lady would afterwards tell Mrs. Harding, or some other friend, that " Heaven alone knew where Frank's money went—not on their dinners, my dear, for they're positively mean."

Nor with her husband's friends did Barbara make a very favourable impression. They admired her, of course; to withhold that tribute was impossible; but they were so utterly different in manner and expression, had such different topics of conversation and such totally opposite opinions to any thing she had even seen or heard, that she sat in silence before them; uttered vague and irrational replies to questions put to her while her thoughts were far away, smiled feebly at wrong times, and so conducted herself, that Mr. M'Malthus, a clever Scotchman, who was worming his way into literature, and was at that time getting a name for blunt offensive sayings (an easily-earned capital, on which many a man has lived for years), was reported to have remarked that "a prettier woman or a bigger fool than Mrs. Churchill was not often seen."

There were others who, while they allowed that she had plenty of common sense (and indeed on occasion, in a cut-and-thurst argument, Barbara showed herself cunning of fence, and by no means deficient in repartee), would call her stuck-up and proud; and there were some, indeed, who repudiated the mere fact of her having lived in a different class of society to which they were not admitted, as in itself an insult and a shame. And even those who were disposed to soften all defects and to exaggerate all virtues—and they were by no means few in number—failed to what they called "get on" with the new Mrs. Churchill. They had no subjects of conversation in common; for even when literary subjects were introduced, they frightened Barbara by their iconoclastic tendencies; deliberately smashing up all those gods whom she had hitherto been accustomed to reverence, and erecting in their stead images inscribed with names unknown to her, or known but to be shuddered at as owned by Radicals or free-thinkers. They were men who outraged none of the social *convénances* of life; about whose manner or behaviour no direct complaint could be made; and often she thought herself somewhat exacting when she would repeat to herself, as she would—oh, how often!—that they were not gentlemen: not her style of gentlemen; that is to say, not the style of men to whom she had been accustomed. When, for instance, would a man have dared to address his conversation to any other man in preference to her, she being present? When could a man have permitted her to open a door, or place a chair for herself, in that set amongst which she had previously moved? Respect her! Her husband's friends would ignore her presence; saying, in reply to a remark from her, " Look here, Churchill, you understand this;" or would prevent her interrupting them (a favourite practice of hers) by putting up their hands and saying, " Pardon me while I state my case," continue their argument in the most dogged manner.

What most amazed Barbara was the calm manner in which all her sallies, however bitter or savage, were received by her husband's intimates, and laughed away or glossed over by Frank himself. At first her notion was to put down these persons by a calm haughty superiority or a studied reticence, which should in itself have the effect of showing her opinion of them: but neither demeanour had the smallest effect on those whom it was intended to reprove. The first time she ever perceived that any one was the least degree inclined to oppose her sway or dispute her authority, was one Saturday night, when Churchill's study was filled with several of his old friends, smoking and chatting. Barbara was there too, with her embroidery. She could stand tobacco-smoke perfectly; it did not give her a headache, or even worse than that, redden her eyelids and make her wink; and there was a small amount of "fastness" in it which pleased her. Moreover her presence prevented the gathering in the *tabagie* from quite sinking into a bachelor revel, the which Barbara, as a young married woman, held in the deepest abomination. The conversation was in full swing about books, authors, and publishers.

"Chester's going to bring out a volume of poems," said Mr. Bloss, an amiable young man with fluffy hair, who always had a good word for every one. "Says he should have published them before, but he's so many irons in the fire."

"Better put his poems where his irons are," laughed Mr. Dunster, a merry little old gentleman with light-blue eyes, who could take the skin off your back and plant daggers in your heart, smiling all the time in the pleasantest manner. "Chester's next door to an idiot; lives close by you, by the way, Bloss, doesn't he?"

"All the men laughed; and even Barbara, after a look of amazement, could not help smiling.

"He's dreadfully frightened of the critics," said another man sitting by. "You must notice him in the *Statesman* yourself, Churchill, eh?"

"Or I'll speak to Harding. Poor Chester! he mustn't be allowed to come to grief. What are his verses like? has any one seen them?"

"I have," said Mr. Bloss. "They're really—

they're — well — they're not so very bad, you know."

"What a burst of candour!" said Mr. Dunster. "Bloss, you are a young reviewer, and I must caution you against such excessively strong statements."

"Chester's most afraid of the *Scourge*," said the man who had spoken before; "he thinks it will flay him."

"He should mollify them by saying that his verses were written 'at an early age,' " laughed Churchill.

"That wouldn't do for the *Scourge*; they would say the verses were too bad even to have been written by a child in arms," said Mr. Dunster.

"How *very* nice! What an old dear you are, Dunster!" said a gentleman sitting in a corner of the fireplace exactly opposite Barbara, with his legs stretched out on a stool, and his body reclining on an easy-chair. This was Mr. Lacy, an artist, who, as it was, made a very good income, but who might have taken the highest rank had his perseverance been on a par with his talent; a sleepy, dreamy man, with an intense appreciation of and regard for himself.

"What do you think of all this, Mrs. Churchill?" asked Bloss; "they are any thing but compassionate in their remarks."

"They may be or not," said Barbara, wearily. "It is all Greek to me: while these gentlemen talk what I believe is called 'shop,' I am utterly unable to follow the conversation."

Frank looked uneasily across at his wife, but said nothing.

"What shall we talk about, Mrs. Churchill?" said Mr. Dunster, with an evil twinkle of his blue eyes. "Shall it be the last ball in the Belgravia, or the new *jupe;* how Mario sang in the *Prophète,* or whether bonnets will be worn on or off the head?"

Churchill frowned at this remark, but his brow cleared as Barbara said with curling lip:

"You need not go so far for illustrations of what you don't understand, Mr. Dunster. Let us discuss tolerance, domestic enjoyments, or the pleasure of being liked by any one,—all of which are, I am sure, equally strange to you."

Mr. Dunster winced, and the fire faded out of his blue eyes: he did not understand being bearded. Frank Churchill, though astonished at seeing his wife defiant, was by no means displeased. Old Mr. Lacy, fearing a storm, which would have ruffled him sadly, struck in at once:

"It's a mistake, my dear Churchill; I'm convinced of it. We're not fit for these charming creatures, we artists and writers, believe me. We're a deucedly irritable, growling, horrible set of ruffians, who ought to be left, like a lot of Robinson Crusoes, each on a separate island. I can fully enter into Mrs. Churchill's feelings; and I've no doubt that Mrs. Lacy feels exactly the same. But what do I do? I'm compelled to shut the door in Mrs. Lacy's face—to lock Mrs. Lacy out. She's a most excellent woman, as you know, Churchill; but she always wants to talk to me when I ought to be at work; now, on a sky-day, for instance! There are very few days in the year in this detestable climate, my dear Mrs. Churchill, which permit of one's seeing the sky sufficiently to paint it. When such a day does happen, I go to my studio and lock the door; but I've scarcely set my palette, before they come and rap, and want to talk to me— to ask me about the butcher, or to tell me about the nurse's sister, or something; and I'm obliged to whistle or sing to prevent my hearing 'em, or I should get interested about the nurse's sister, and open the door, and then my day's work would be spoilt."

"You're right, Lacy," said Dunster: "men who've got work to do should remain single. They'll never—"

"Come, you're polite to my wife," said Frank. "This is flat blasphemy against the state into which we've just entered."

"Oh, pray don't let the conversation, evidently so genial, be stopped on my account. I'm tired, and am just going;" and with a sweeping bow Barbara sailed out of the room.

An hour afterwards, when Frank looked in from his dressing-room, he saw in the dim light Barbara's hair streaming over the pillow, and going to her found traces of tears on her cheeks. Tenderly and eagerly he asked her what had happened.

"Oh, Frank, Frank!" she exclaimed, bursting into fresh sobs; "I see it all now! What those horrid men said is too true! We were worse than mad to marry. Your friends will never understand me, while I shall interfere with your work and your pleasure; and, oh! I am so very, very miserable myself!"

CHAPTER V.

THE FLYBYNIGHTS.

To such of womankind as knew of its existence
there were few places in London so thoroughly un-
popular as the Flybynights Club. And yet it was
an unpretending little room, boasting none of the
luxury of decoration generally associated in the
female mind with notions of club-life, and offering
no inducement for membership save that it was
open at very abnormal hours, and that it was
very select. The necessary qualification for can-
didature was that you should be somebody; no
matter what your profession (provided, of course,
that you were a gentleman by position), you must
have made some mark in it, shown yourself ahead
of the ruck of competitors, before you could have
been welcome among the Flybynights. Two or
three leading advocates, attached for the most part

to the criminal bar; half-a-dozen landscape and
figure painters of renown; half-a-dozen actors; a
sporting man or two, with the power of talking
about something else besides Brother to Bluenose's
performances; two or three City men, who combined the most thorough business habits with convivial tastes in the " off" hours; a few members of
Parliament, who were compelled to respect the
room as a thoroughly neutral ground; a few jour-
nalists and authors, and a sprinkling of nothing-
doing men about town,—formed the corporate body
of the club. What was its origin? I believe that
certain members of the Haresfoot Club, finding
that establishment scarcely so convivial as report
had led them to believe; that the *Dii majores* of
the house were a few snuffy old gentlemen, without
an idea beyond the assertion of their own dignity,
and the keeping up of some dreary fictions and
time-worn conventionalities; that the delights of
the smoking-room, so much talked of in the outer
world, in reality consisted in sitting between a
talkative barrister and a silent stockbroker, or
listening to the complaints against the manage-

ment of the club by the committee;—finding, in fact, that the place was dull, bethought them of establishing another where they could be more amused. Hence the Flybynights.

The Flybynights had no house of their own;. they merely occupied a room on the basement of the Orpheus tavern,—a dull sombre old room, with big couches and lounges covered with frayed leather, with a smoky old green-flock paper, and with no ornament save a battered old looking-glass in a fly-blown frame. Occasionally roysterers new to town, on their way to the big concert-room of the Orpheus, where they were to be enchanted with the humour of Mr. Bloss's "Dying Cadger's Lament," or the pathos of Mr. Seeinault's "Trimbuilt Wherry," would in mistake push open the green-baize door leading to the Flybynights sanctum, and immediately withdraw in dismay at the dinginess of the room and the grim aspect of its occupants. That grimness, however, was only assumed at the apparition of a stranger; when the members were alone among themselves, perfect freedom from restraint was the rule. And if, on the next morning, the jurymen who listened with awe to the withering denunciations which fell from the lips of the learned counsel for the prosecution,—the bank-directors who nodded approval to the suggestions of certain shrewd financiers,—the noble sitters who marked the brows of the artists engaged on their portraits, "sicklied o'er with the pale cast of thought,"—nay, even the patients who gazed with eager eyes to glean something from the countenances of the physicians then clutching their pulses,—had seen counsel, financiers, artists, and physicians on the previous evening at the Flybynights, they could not have recognised them for the same men. The fame of the club spread; anecdotes and *bon-mots* ran round town more quickly, and were better received, when they had the Flybynight stamp. It was rumoured that O'Blank and Macaster, the great authors, were occasionally to be seen there in the flesh, conversing like ordinary mortals; heavy swells found out that it was open as late as Pratt's, and asked each other, in elliptic phraseology, "Whether 'twasn't good kind place, eh? met 'musing kind fellahs there;

made laugh'n, that kind thing?" But though they made various attempts at election, they never got beyond an occasional visit to the club; friendly attempts to smuggle them in as members were dead failures; and at every ballot, generally held at midnight, the strident voice of Rupert Robinson, author and dramatist, could be heard asking, at the mention of any candidate's name, "Who is he? what can he do? what has he done?" questions which, unless satisfactorily answered, caused the immediate pilling of the pretender to association with the Flybynights.

A few weeks after the Schröders' reception, Beresford and Simnel, who had been dining together, strolled into the club soon after midnight. Beresford was a member; Simnel came as his guest; the latter would have been safe of election, as his tact and shrewdness were very generally known and highly esteemed amongst the men, but he always refused to be put in nomination. "It's all very well for Beresford," he would say; "he's a Commissioner, and can do as he likes; I'm an upper servant; and though you're a deuced pleasant

set of fellows, you haven't got a great name for
respectability with the B. P., or British Public,
whom I serve. It's horribly virtuous, is the B. P.,
and is always in bed before you sweet youths meet
in this bower of bliss. So that though I'm delighted
to come occasionally with Charley and pay you a
visit, I must be in a position, if called upon, to
swear that I'm not an affiliated member of your
sacred brotherhood." The other men understood
all this, and liked Simnel better for his candour;
and there was no visitor at the Flybynights more
welcome than he. It was a great occasion at the
Flybynights; one of the members, Mr. Plinlimmon
the poet, had that day been giving a lecture " On
Sentiment, its Use and Abuse," at St. Cecilia's
Hall, and had had great success. For Mr. Plinlimmon was not a mere common poet who made
verses and sold them; he was cousin to Lady Heri-
tage, whose husband was the Lord Privy-Purse;
and he was very well off, and wrote only for his
amusement, and consequently was the very man to
be patronised. Moreover, he wrote weak little verse-
lets, like very-much-diluted Wordsworth, abound-

ing in passages quotable for Academy pictures of bread-and-butter children ; and he was much taken up by Mr. Spicklittle, the editor of the *Boomerang Magazine*, so soon as it was understood that he stood well with the fashionable world. And there had been a very fashionable audience at St. Cecilia's Hall to hear Mr. Plinlimmon on " Sentiment," and the stalls had been filled with what was afterwards stated in the public prints to be the rank and flower of the land ; and high-born women had complimented him on the conclusion of his labours, and had voted his lecture charming : all of which thoroughly consoled the lecturer, and enabled him to forget the rude conduct of certain rough-spoken critics in the body of the hall, who had loudly cried " Bosh !" at his finest passages, and gone out with much shuffling of thick boots and dropping of heavy walking-sticks long before his peroration. And after dining with a countess, Mr. Plinlimmon thought that the right thing was to go down and show himself at the Flybynights Club, of which he was a member ; and he had entered the room just before Beresford and Simnel arrived.

"Hail, Plinlimmon!" shouted Mr. Magnus the historian, with kindly glances beaming through his spectacles; "hail, bard of the what-d'ye-call-it! How air you, colonel?"

"Hallo, Plinlimmon!" said Mr. Rupert Robinson; "been giving a show, haven't you? what sort of house did you have? who looked after your checks? you were very well billed, I noticed."

Plinlimmon shuddered.

"Lecturing, haven't you?" asked Mr. Slater, critic of the *Moon*.

"Yes," said Plinlimmon, "I have been giving a lecture."

"Ah!" said Mr. Schrink, critic of the *Statesman*, "if I'm not wrong, Dr. Johnson defines the verb to lecture as to 'instruct insolently and dogmatically.' You're quite capable of that, Plinlimmon."

"What was your subject, sir?" asked Mr. Mugg, low comedian of the Sanspareil Theatre.

"Sentiment, sir!" said Mr. Plinlimmon fiercely; it began to dawn on him that he was being chaffed.

"Deary me!" said Mr. Mugg, with feigned won
der and uplifted hands; "sentiment, eh? them's
my sentiments!"

"Silence, you ribalds!" said Mr. Magnus.
"You had a large attendance, I hear, Plinlimmon;
more women than men, though, I suppose? Men
don't come in the day-time."

"There was a great gathering of the female
aristocracy," said Plinlimmon, perking up his head.

"One old woman jawing always brings together a lot of others," growled Mr. Dunster,
beneath his breath. He had been apparently doz-
ing in a far corner of the room, but had roused
up at the word "aristocracy,"—as sure an irritant
to him as a red rag to a bull,—and his bright blue
eyes were gleaming.

"I didn't think much of your delivery, Plinlimmon," said Mr. Slater.

"It was as slow as a mid-day postman's, and
not so sure," said Mr. Schrink; "you got uncommonly drowsy and bag-pipy at times."

"I'll tell you what it is, Plinlimmon," said
Mr. Dunster; "you are uncommonly dreary!

You're a swell, and you can't help it; but you were horribly slow. I'll tell you what it is, my young friend; you're far too dull by yourself,— *you want a piano!*"

During the roar which followed this remark, Beresford felt a light touch on his arm, and turning round saw Dr. Prater.

Not to be known to Dr. Prater was to confess that the "pleasure of your acquaintance" was of little value; for assuredly, had it been worth any thing, Dr. Prater would have had it by hook or by crook. A wonderful man, Dr. Prater, who had risen from nothing, as his detractors said; but however that might be, he had a practice scarcely excelled by any in London. Heart and lungs were Dr. Prater's specialities; and persons imagining themselves afflicted in those regions came from all parts of England, and thronged the doctor's dining-room in Queen-Anne Street in the early forenoons, vainly pretending to read Darwin *On the Fertilisation of Orchids,* the *Life of Captain Hedley Vicars,* or the Supplement of yesterday's *Times;* and furtively glancing round at the other occupants of the room, and wondering what was the matter with them. That dining-room looked rather different about a dozen times in the season, of an evening, when the books were cleared away, and the big bronze gas-chandelier lighted, and the doctor sat at the large round-table surrounded by a dozen of the pleasantest people in London. Such a mixture! Never was such a man for " bringing people together" as Dr. Prater. The manager of the Italian Opera (Dr. Prater's name was to all the sick-certificates for singers) would be seated next to a judge, who would have a leading member of the Jockey Club on his other hand, and a bishop for his *vis-à-vis*. Next the bishop would be a cotton-lord, next to him the artist of a comic periodical, and next to him a rising member of the Opposition, with an Indian colonel and an American comedian, here on a starring engagement, in juxtaposition. The dinner was always good, the wines excellent, and the doctor was the life and soul of the party. He had something special to say to every one; and as his big protruding eyes shone and glimmered through his gold-rimmed spectacles, he looked like a convivial little owl. A very different man over the dinner-table to the smug little pale-faced man in black, whom wretched patients found in the morning sitting behind a leather-covered table, on which a stethoscope was conspicuously displayed, and who, after sounding the chests of consumptive curates or struggling clerks, would say, with an air of blandness, dashed with sorrow, " I'm afraid the proverbially treacherous air of our climate will not do for us, my dear sir! I'm afraid we must spend our winter at Madeira, or at least at Pau. *Good* day to you ;" and then the doctor, after shaking hands with his patient, would slip the tips of his fingers into his trousers-pockets, into which would fall another little paper-package to join a number already there deposited, while the curate or clerk, whose yearly income was perhaps two hundred pounds, and who probably had debts amounting to twice his annual earnings, would go away wondering whether it was better to endeavour to borrow the further sum necessary at ruinous interest, or to go back and die in the cold Lincolnshire clay parish, or in the bleak Northern city, as the case might be. On one thing the doctor prided himself greatly, that he never let a patient know what he thought of him. He would bid a man remove his waistcoat with a semi-jocund air, and the next instant listen to a peculiar "click" inside his frame, which betrayed the presence of heart-disease liable at any moment to carry the man off, without altering a muscle of his face or a tone of his voice. "Hum! ha! we must be a little careful; we must not expose ourselves to the night-air! Take a leetle more care of yourself, my dear sir; for instance, I would wear a wrap round the throat—some wrap, you know, to prevent the cold striking to the part affected. Send this to Bell's, and get it made up, and take it three times a-day; and let me see you on—on Saturday. *Good* day to you." And there would not be the smallest quiver in the hard metallic voice, or the smallest twinkle in the observant eye behind the gold-rimmed glasses, although the doctor knew that the demon Consumption, by his buffet, had raised that red spot on the sufferer's cheek, and was rapidly eating away his vitality.

But if Dr. Prater kept a strict reticence to his patients as regarded their own ailments, he was never so happy as when enlarging to them on the diseases of their fellow-sufferers, or of informing esoteric circles of the special varieties of disorder with which his practice led him to cope. "*You* ill, my dear sir!" he would say to some puny specimen; then, settling himself into his waist-coat after examination, "*you* complain of narrow-chestedness,—why, my dear sir, do you know Sir Hawker de la Crache? You've a pectoral development which is perfectly surprising when contrasted with Sir Hawker's. But then he, poor man! last stage,—Madeira no good,—would sit up all night playing whist at Reid's Hotel. Algiers no good,—too much brandy, tobacco, and *baccarat* with French officers—nothing any good. *You*, my dear sir, compared to Sir Hawker—pooh, nonsense!" Or in another form: "Any such case, my dear madam? any such case?"—turning to a large book, having previously consulted a small index—"a hundred such! Here, for instance, Lady Susan Bray, now staying at Ventnor, living entirely on asses'-milk—in some of our conditions we must live on asses'-milk— left lung quite gone, life hanging by a thread. You're a Juno, ma'am, in comparison to Lady Susan!" There was no mistake, however, about the doctor's talent; men in his own profession, who sneered at his *charlatanerie* of manner, allowed that he was thoroughly well versed in his subject. He was very fond of young men's society; and, with all his engagements, always found time to dine occasionally with the Guards at Windsor, with a City Company or two, or with a snug set *en petit comité* in Temple chambers, and to visit the behind-scenes of two or three theatres, the receptions of certain great ladies, and occasionally the meetings of the Flybynights Club. To the latter he always came in a special suit of clothes on account of the impregnation of tobacco-smoke; and when coming thither he left his carriage and his address, in case he was required, at the Minerva, with orders to fetch him at once.

It would never have done for some of his patients to know that he was a member of the Flybynights.

Such was Dr. Prater, who touched Beresford on the arm and said, "Not again, my dear sir! I will not be balked of the opportunity of saying, 'how d'ye do?' to you again."

"Ah, doctor," said Beresford with that apparent frankness and *bonhomie* to which he owed so much of his popularity, "delighted to see you! But what do you mean 'balked of the opportunity'? Where was that?"

"A few weeks since, just before I left town; —I've been away, and Dr. Seaton has kindly attended to my practice;—we met at the house of our charming friend Mrs. Schröder; but I could not catch your eye. You were too well engaged; there was, as somebody—I don't know who, but somebody that every one knows—has said, there was metal more attractive. Ha! ha! A charming woman, Mrs. Schröder! a very charming woman!"

"Very charming," echoed Mr. Beresford shortly, not particularly caring about finding himself thoroughly focussed by the doctor's sharpest glances concentrated through his spectacles. "By the way, don't you know our secretary, Mr. Simnel, Dr. Prater?"

The gentlemen bowed. "I have the pleasure of being well acquainted with Mr. Simnel by name, and of being at the present moment engaged in a correspondence with him in reference to a certificate which I have given. And, by the way, my dear sir," turning to Simnel, "you really must give young Pierrepoint his six weeks. You must indeed?"

"If it rested with me, doctor, I'd give him unlimited leave; confer on him the order of the 'sack,'" said Simnel, bluntly—"an idle stuck-up young hound!"

"Harsh words, my dear sir; harsh words! However, I will leave our young friend's case with you and Mr. Beresford; I am sure it could not be in better hands. You were not in Saxe-Coburg Square the other night, I think? De-lightful party!"

"No," said Simnel, "I'm not a great evening-party man myself; it's only your butterflies of fashion, like our friend here, who enjoy those light and airy gaieties. My pleasures are of a more substantial kind. By the way, doctor, how's Kitty Vavasour's cough?"

The doctor's eyes twinkled as he replied, "Oh, much better—very much better. Horrible draught down that first entrance, my dear sir, as she perhaps told—I mean, as you probably know. Dreadful draught! enough to kill half the *coryphées* in London. I've spoken to Grabb about it, but he won't do any thing; and when I hinted at the drapery, asked me if I thought he was going to let his ballet-girls dance in bathing-gowns. Very rude man, Grabb."

"Very good style they did that in the other night," said Beresford, cutting in—"in Saxe-Coburg Square, I mean-—very good, was'nt it? I suppose it was the lady's taste; but when they get hold of a woman with any notion of arrangement and effect, these *parvenu* fellows from the City certainly don't grudge the money for their fun. And in the way the Schröders are living, the establishment must cost a pretty sum, I should imagine."

"A pretty sum indeed, my dear sir," said the doctor. "However, I understand on all sides that Mr. Schröder can perfectly afford it. I hear from those who ought to know" (a great phrase of Dr. Prater's, this) "that his income is princely!" And then the doctor looked at the other two and repeated "princely!" and smacked his lips as though the word had quite a nice taste in his mouth.

"It's a good thing to be a Polish Jew," growled Mr. Simnel. "This fellow's ancestors lent money to long-haired Grafs and swaggering Electors, and got their interest when they could; and thought themselves deuced lucky not to get their teeth pulled out when they asked for a little on account, or not to be put on the fire when they presented their bill. Their descendant lives in pleasanter days; we've given up pulling out their teeth, worse luck! And that neat little instrument, 'Victoria, by the grace,' is as open to Jews as Christians. I always thought there was something wrong in that."

“This Schröder is a tremendously lucky fellow, by Jove!” said Beresford. “He’s got a very pretty wife and an enormous fortune; and though he’s not young, to judge from all appearances, has a constitution of iron, and will live for years to enjoy his good fortune.”

“Ah, my dear sir,” said Dr. Prater in a low and solemn voice, “I’m afraid you’re not correct in one particular; not correct in one particular!” and the little man shook his head and looked specially oracular.

Simnel glanced up at him at once from under his heavy eyebrows; but Beresford only said, “Why, doctor, you’re not going to try and make me believe any envious disparagement of Schröder’s riches?”

“Not for the world, my dear sir; not for the world! Such rumours have been spread! but, as you say, only among the envious and jealous, who would whisper-away Coutts’s credit, and decline to intrust their miserable balance to Barings’! No; my doubts as to Schröder related to another matter.”

"His health?" said Simnel, who had kept his eyes on the solemn little man, and was regarding him keenly.

"Pre-cisely!" said the doctor. And he stepped aside for an instant, helped himself to a pinch of snuff from a box on a neighbouring table, and returned to his companions, gazing up at them with a solemn steady stare that made him look more like an owl than ever.

"His health!" exclaimed Beresford, "why, there's surely nothing the matter with that! He has the chest of a horse and the digestion of an ostrich. I don't know a man of his age to whom, to look at, you'd give a longer life."

"Right, my dear sir," replied the doctor, "right enough from a non-professional view. But Mr. Schröder, like the gentleman of whom I have heard, but whose name I can't call to mind, has that within which passeth show. I *know* the exact state of his condition."

"This is very interesting," said Mr. Simnel, drawing closer to the doctor on the ottoman; "very interesting, indeed; yours is a wonderful profession, doctor, for gaining insight into men and things. Would it be too much to ask you to tell us a little more about this particular case?"

"Well, you know, I don't often talk of these matters; there *are* men in our profession, my dear sir, who gossip and chatter, and I believe make it pay very well; but they are men of no intellect, mere quacks and charlatans—quacks and charlatans! But with gentlemen like yourselves, men of the world, I don't mind occasionally revealing a few of the secrets of the—the—what d'ye call 'em? —prison-house. The fact is—" and the doctor lowered his voice and looked additionally solemn,— "that Mr. Schröder's life hangs by a thread."

Both his listeners started and Mr. Simnel from between his set teeth said, "The devil!"

"By a thread!" repeated the doctor, holding out his finger and thumb as though he actually had the thread between them. "He may go off at any moment; his life is not certain for an hour; he's engaged, as you know, in tremendous transactions, and any sudden fright or passion would be his certain death."

" Ah, then his disease is—"

" Heart, my dear sir, heart !" said the doctor; tapping himself on the left side of his waistcoat, " his heart's diseased,—one cannot exactly say how far, but I suspect strongly,—and he may go out at any moment like the snuff of a candle."

" Have you known this long?" asked Beresford.

" Only two days : he came to me two days ago to consult me about a little worrying cough which he described himself as having; and in listening at his chest I heard the death-beat. No mistaking it, my dear sir; when you've once heard that ' click,' you never forget it."

" By Jove, how horrible !" said Simnel.

" Poor devil ! does he know it himself?" asked Beresford.

" Know it, my dear sir ? Of course not. You don't imagine *I* told him ? Why, the shock might have killed him on the spot. Oh, dear, no ! I prescribed for his cough, and told him specially to avoid all kind of excitement : that was the only warning I dare give him."

As the doctor said this, Mr. Simnel rose. "It's a horrible idea," said he with a shudder— "horrible !"

"Very common, my dear sir, very common. If you knew how many men there are whom I meet out at dinner, in society, here and there, whom I know to be as distinctly marked for death as if I saw the plague-spot on their breasts !"

"Well, you've completely frightened me," said Beresford. "I'll get home to bed, and try and forget it in sleep. Are you coming, Simnel? Good-night, doctor." And the two gentlemen went out together, leaving the little doctor already sidling up to another group.

When they were out in the street, and had started on their homeward walk, Simnel said to his companion :

"That was strange news we've just heard."

"Strange, indeed," replied Beresford. "Do you think the doctor's right?"

"Not a doubt of it; he's a garrulous idiot; as full of talk as an old woman; but I have always heard very skilful in his profession, and in this special disease I believe there are none to beat him. Oh, yes, he's right enough. Well, you always held winning cards, and now the game looks like yours."

"Simnel," said Beresford, stopping short and looking up into his face, "what the devil do you mean?"

"Mean!" echoed Simnel; "I'll tell you when you come on; it's cold stopping still in the streets, and the policeman at the corner is staring at you in unmitigated wonder. Mean!" he repeated, as they walked on; "well, it's not a very difficult matter to explain. You hear that Schröder has heart-disease—that at any moment he may die. You always had a partiality for Mrs. Schröder, I believe; and if there be any truth in what I gather from yourself and others, you stand very well with her."

"Well?"

"Well! You're dense to-night, Master Charley. Well? Why, you've as great a chance as man ever had before you. You've only to wait until what Prater told us of happens,—and if he's right, it won't be long,—and then marry the widow and start as a millionaire."

" By Jove, it *is* a great chance !" said Beresford, looking at his friend.

" And yet you didn't see it until just now. Why, it opened straight up in front of me the instant that chattering medico mentioned the fact. If you play your cards well, you're all right ; but, remember, flirtation and courtship are two different things, and must be managed differently. And recollect it's for the latter you're now going in. Now, here's my street, so adieu. Sleep on this matter, and we'll talk of it to-morrow morning.

" It's a tremendous fluke," said Mr. Simnel, as he leisurely undressed himself; " but it will serve my purpose admirably. That eight hundred pounds of mine lent to Master Charley looks much less shaky than it did, and what a trump-card to play with Kate !"

CHAPTER VI.

MR. SIMNEL AT THE DEN.

Two days after the events recorded in the last chapter, Mr. Simnel left the Tin-Tax Office a couple of hours earlier than his usual time of departure, and taking a cab, hurried off to his apartments in Piccadilly. Overlooking the Green Park, sufficiently lofty to be removed from the immediate noise of the traffic, and situate in that part of the street which was macadamised, there were, perhaps, no more delightful chambers in town than those occupied by the Tin-Tax secretary. They consisted but of three rooms—sitting-room, bed-chamber, and bath-room; but all were lofty and well-proportioned, and were furnished in a thoroughly luxurious manner. A big book-case, with its contents admirably selected, covered one side of the sitting-room, on the walls of which hung Raphael Morghen prints, and before-letter proofs after Landseer, Leslie, and Stan-field; a round table, over which were suspended three swinging moderator-lamps, with white-china shades and crimson-silk fringe; a sofa and nu-merous easy-chairs, all in crimson velvet and wal-nut-wood; rich spoils of Bohemian glass, standing in odd corners on quaint oak cabinets; two Sèvres china dogs, in begging attitude, mounting guard on either end of the mantleshelf; and a flying female figure suspended across the looking-glass; —such were among the incongruous contents of the room. On the table, two yellow-paper covered French novels, a Horace, and M'Culloch's Com-mercial Directory lay side by side; in the look-ing-glass, cards for evening-parties and dinners were jostled by tickets soliciting vote and interest in approaching elections of charitable societies, remindings of gatherings of learned bodies, and small bills for books or boots. It was Mr. Simnel's pleasure to keep up this *melange;* his time was generally fully occupied; he chose people to con-sider that he had not a moment to himself; he

wished those who called on him on business to see
the invitations, in order that they might judge
therefrom of his position in society; and he took
care that the attention of those idle droppers-in,
who came on a Sunday morning, for instance, or
late at night, to have a chat, should be directed
to the business-cards, to give them a notion of
his standing in the money-making, business world.
Since Mr. Simnel assumed the reins at the Tin-
Tax Office, two or three hundred men had sat with
their legs under that round table, discussing an
excellent dinner, and meeting pleasant people; but
not one of them had ever left the room without
Mr. Simnel's feeling that his coming had been
productive of benefit to his host, and that the invitation had fully answered its intent.   Baron
Oppenhardt, the great financier, never could tell
what made him accept Simnel's invitation, save
that he knew his host was connected with Government and had a long head of his own; yet he
never refused.   And little Blurt, whose " connexion with the press" was of a limited nature,
never could understand why, biennially, he sat

under those shaded moderator-lamps in Piccadilly, and consumed Pommery Greno out of bell-shaped glasses. But Simnel knew why he had them to dinner, and took their value both out of Oppenhardt and Blurt.

A long-headed man, Mr. Simnel, and, to judge from the strange smile on his face on that particular day, full of some special scheme, as he emerged from his bed-room and looked out into Piccadilly. Any thing but a vain man, and long past the age when the decoration of one's person enters largely into account, Mr. Simnel had yet paid special attention to his toilette during the short interval which had elapsed since his arrival at home from the Tin-Tax Office. He was got up with elaborate care and yet perfect simplicity; indeed, there was a touch of the old school in his drab riding-trousers, white waistcoat, blue cutaway coat, and blue bird's-eye neckerchief, with small stand-up collars. A glance into the street showed him that his horses were ready, and he descended at once. At the door he found his groom mounted on a knowing-looking gray cob, short, stiff, and sturdy, and leading a splendid thoroughbred bright bay with black points. This Mr. Simnel mounted and rode easily away.

Through Decimus Burton's archway he turned into Hyde Park and made at once for the Row. There were but few men lounging about there at that time of the year, but Simnel was known to some of them; and after nods had been exchanged, they fell to comparing notes about him and his horse and his style of living, wondering how it was done, admiring his cleverness, detracting from his position—talking, in fact, as men will do of another who has beat them in this grand struggle for place which we call life. The Row was very empty, and Simnel paid but little attention to its occupants: now and then he occasionally raised his whip mechanically in acknowledgment of some passing salute, but it is to be doubted whether he knew to whom he was telegraphing, as his thoughts were entirely fixed on his mission. However, he wore a pleasant smile on his face, and that was quite enough: grinning, like charity, covers a multitude of sins; and if you only smile and hold your tongue, you can pass through life with an *éclat* which excellent eloquence, combined with a serious face, would fail to give. So **Mr.** Simnel went smiling along at the easiest amble until he got clear of the Row and the town, and then he gave the bay his head, and never drew rein until he turned up a country lane immediately on passing Ealing Common.

Half way up this lane stood The Den, and evidences of Kate Mellon's calling began to abound so soon as you turned out of the high-road. In the fields on either side through the bare hedges one could see a string of horses in cloths and head-pieces, each ridden by a groom, skirting the hedges along which a proper riding-path had been made; occasionally a yellow break, driven by a veteran coachman, with a younger and more active coadjutor perched up behind, and standing with his eyes on a level with the coach-box observing every motion of the horses, would rumble by, while the clay-coloured gig containing **Mr.** Sandcrack the veterinary surgeon, who, in his long white cravat, beard, and tight trousers, looked a pleasant compound of a dissenting-minister, a horse-jockey, and an analytical chemist, was flying in and out of the lane at all times and seasons. Mr. Simnel seemed accustomed to these scenes and thoroughly well known amongst them, the grooms and breaksmen touched their hats to him, and he exchanged salutations with Mr. Sandcrack, and told him that the bay had got rid of all his wind-galls and never went better in his life. So straight up the lane until he arrived at the lodge, and then, before his groom could ride up, his cheery cry of " Gate !" brought out the buxom lodge-keeper, and she also greeted Mr. Simnel with a curtsey of recognition, and received his largesse as he rode through; so down the little carriage-drive, past the pigeon-house elevated on a pole, and the pointers' kennels, and the strip of garden cultivated by the lodge-keeper, and in which one of the lodge-keeper's dirty chubby children was always sprawling; past the inner gates, through which could be caught glimpses of the circular straw-ride, and the stable and loose boxes, and the neatly gravelled court-yard, up the sweep and so to the house-door. Freeman, the staid stud-groom from Yorkshire, had seen the visitor's entry from the stable, where he was superintending, and hurried up to meet him. Before Mr. Simnel's own groom had come alongside, Freeman was at his horse's head.

"Mornin', sir," said he, touching his hat. "Missis is oop at Fouracres, close by, givin' lesson to a young leddy, just by t' water soide: joompin' brook, oi think. Howsever she'll be in d'rackly, oi know."

"All right, Freeman," said Mr. Simnel, leisurely dismounting. "Horses all well? Fine weather for horseflesh, this!"

"Ay, ay, it be, sir!" said the old man. "Stood be pratty well, oi'm thinkin': coughs and colds, and that loike, as is allays case this toime o' year."

"Don't hurry Miss Mellon on my account, Freeman," said Mr. Simnel; "I can wait. I'll go into the house, and you can let her know that I'm here, when she comes in. By the way, Freeman, I haven't seen you since Christmas: here's for old acquaintance' sake."

Freeman touched his hat gratefully, but not submissively, as he pocketed the half-sovereign which Mr. Simnel slipped into his capacious palm, and moved off towards the stables with the groom and the horses.

" Good man, that," said Simnel to himself, as he went into the house. " Straightforward, conscientious sort of fellow, and thoroughly devoted to *her*. Proper style of man to have in an establishment: thoroughly respectable—do one credit by his looks. If it ever comes off, I certainly should keep Mr. Freeman on."

Mr. Simnel passed on into the long low dining-room, where he found the table spread for luncheon, with a very substantial display of cold roast beef, fowls, and tongue, sherry, and a tall bottle of German wine. He smiled as he noticed these preparations, and then leisurely walked round the room. He paused at an oil-painting of Kate with a favourite horse by her side. The artist evidently knew much more about the equine than the human race. The horse's portrait was admirable, but poor Kitty, with vermilion cheeks and glaring red hair, and a blue habit with long daubs of light in it, like rain-streaks on a window, was a lamentable object to look on. Only one other picture decorated the walls, a portrait of the Right Hon. the Earl of Quorn, aged 61, founder of the Society for the Relief of Incapacitated Jobmasters and Horse-dealers, dedicated to him by his faithful servants the publishers; representing a hale old gentleman, remarkable principally for his extraordinary length of check-neckcloth, seated on a weight-carrying cob, and staring intently at nothing. On a side-table lay a thick book, *Youatt on the Horse*, and a thin pamphlet, *Navicular not Incurable*, a *Little Warbler* (Poor Kitty!), and a kind of album, into which a heterogeneous mixture of recipes for horse-medicines, scraps of hunting news, lists of prices fetched at the sales of celebrated studs, and other sporting memoranda had been pasted. Simnel was looking through this, and had just come upon a slip of printed matter, evidently cut from a newspaper, announcing the appointment of Mr. Charles Beresford to be a commissioner of the Tin-Tax Office, in place of Cockle pensioned—a slip against which there were three huge deep pencil-scorings—when the door opened and his hostess entered.

Although her habit was draggled and splashed, and her hair disarranged and blown about her face, Kate Mellon never had looked, to Simnel's eyes at least, more thoroughly charming than she did at that instant. The exercise she had just gone through had given her a splendid colour, her eyes were bright and sparkling, her whole frame showed to perfection in the tight-fitting jacket; and as she came into the room and removed her hat, the knot of hair behind, loosened from the comb, fell over her shoulders in golden profusion. She wound it up at once with one hand, advancing with the other outstretched to her guest.

"Sorry I'm late, Simnel," said she; "but I'd a pupil here, and business is business, as you know well enough. Can't afford to throw away any chance, so I gave her her hour, and now she's off, and I am all the better by a guinea. I didn't stop to change my habit because I heard you were waiting, and I knew you wouldn't mind."

"You couldn't look more enchanting than you do now, Kate," said Simnel.

"Yes, yes; I know," said Kitty; "all right! But I thought you knew better than that. This is the wrong shop for flummery of that sort; as you ought to have learnt by this time. Have some lunch?"

They sat down to the table, and during the meal talked on ordinary subjects; for the most part discussing their common acquaintance, but always carefully avoiding bringing Beresford's name forward. When they had finished, Kate said, "You want to smoke, of course. I think I shall have a puff myself. No, thank you; your weeds are too big for me; I've got some Queens here that old Sir John Elle sent me after I broke that roan mare for his daughter. By George, what a brute that was! nearly killed me at first, she did; and now you might ride her with a pack-thread."

Simnel did not reply. Kate Mellon curled herself up on an ottoman in the window with her habit tucked round her; lit a small cigar; and slowly expelling the smoke said, as the blue vapour curled round her head, "And now to business! You wanted to talk to me, you said; and I told you to come up to-day. What's it all about?"

"About yourself, Kate. You know thoroughly well my feelings to you; you know how often I have—"

"Hold on a minute!" said Kate; "I know that you've been philandering and hanging on about me,—or would have been, if I'd have let you,—for this year past. I know that well enough; but I thought there was to be none of this. I thought I'd told you to drop that subject, and that you'd consented to drop it. I told you I wouldn't listen to you, and—"

"Why would not you listen to me, Kate?" said Simnel earnestly.

"Why? Because—"

"Don't trouble yourself to find an excuse; I'll tell you why," said Simnel. "Because you were desperately bent on a fruitless errand; because you were beating the wind and trying to check the storm; because you were in love,—I

must speak plainly, Kitty, in a matter like this,—·
in love with a man who did not return your
feeling, and who even now is boasting of your
passion, and laughing at you as its dupe!"

"What!" cried the girl, throwing away the
cigar and starting to her feet.

"Sit down, child," said Simnel, gently laying
his hand on her arm; "sit down, and hear me
out. I know your pluck and spirit; and nothing
grieves me more, or goes more against the grain
with me,' than to have to tell you this. But when
I tell you that the man to whom you so attached
yourself has spoken lightly and sneeringly of
your infatuation; that amongst his friends he has
laughingly talked of a scene which occurred on
the last occasion of his visit to this house, when
you suggested that he should marry you—"

"Did he say that?" asked the girl, pushing
her hair back from her face,—"did he say that?"

"That and more; laughed at the notion,
and—"

"O, my God!" shrieked Kate Mellon, throwing up her arms. "Spare me! stop, for Heaven's

sake, and don't let me hear any more. Did he say that of me? Then they'll all know it, and when I meet them will grin and whisper as I know they do. Haven't I heard them do it of others a thousand times? and now to think they'll have the pull of me. O good Lord, good Lord!" and she burst into tears and buried her face in her handkerchief. Then suddenly rousing, she exclaimed: "What do you come and tell me this for, Simnel? What business is it of yours? What's your motive in coming and smashing me up like this?"

"One, and one only," said Simnel in a low voice. "I wanted to prevent your demeaning yourself by ever showing favour to a man who has treated you so basely. I wanted you to show your own pride and spirit by blotting this Beresford from your thoughts. I wanted you to do this—whatever may be the result—because—I love you, Kate!"

"That's it!" she cried suddenly—"that's it! You're telling me lies and long stories, and breaking my heart, and making me make a fool of myself, only that you may stand well with me and get me to like you! How do I know what you say is true? Why should Charley do this? Why did Charley refuse what I offered him? I meant it honestly enough, God knows. Oh, why did he refuse it?" and again she burst into tears.

"Oh, he did refuse it?" said Simnel, quietly. "So far, then, you see I am right; and you will find I am right throughout. I'll tell you why he acted as he did to you. Because he's full of family pride, and because he never cared for you one rush. At this very moment he is desperately in love with a married woman, and is only awaiting her husband's death to make her his wife!"

"Can you prove that?" asked Kate eagerly.

"I can! You shall have ample opportunity of satisfying yourself—"

"Does the husband suspect?"

"Not in the least."

"That's right!" said the girl with sudden energy—"that'll do! Only let me prove that, and I'll give him up for ever."

"If I do this for you, Kitty, surely my love will be sufficiently proved.   You will then—"

"Yes, we'll talk of that afterwards.   I'll see you next week, and you'll tell me more of this new love-affair of—of *his!*   Don't stop now.   I'm all out of sorts.   You've upset me.   I wasn't in condition.   I've been doing a little too much work lately.   Go now, there's a good fellow!   Good-by."   Then stopping suddenly—"You're sure you're not selling me, Simnel?"

"I swear it!" said Simnel.

"I wish to heaven you had been," said the poor girl; "but we'll see about the new business next week.   I think we'll spoil that pretty game between us, eh?   There, good-by."   And she set her teeth tight, and rushed from the room.

"So far so good," said Mr. Simnel, as he rode quietly home.   "She's taken it almost a little too strongly.   My plan now is to soften her and turn her to me.   I think I have a card in my hand that will win that trick, and then—the game's my own!"

CHAPTER VII.

MR. BERESFORD IN PURSUIT.

THE idea suggested by Simnel, after the interview with Dr. Prater at the Flybynights, came upon Mr. Beresford with extraordinary force. It opened up to him a new train of thought, gave a complete turn to his intended course of life, afforded him matter for the deepest study and reflection. As we have already seen, he was a man with a faultless digestion, and without a scrap of heart—two qualities which had undoubtedly greatly conduced towards his success in life, and towards making him a careless, easy-going, worldly philosopher. When he first saw Miss Townshend at Bissett Grange, he remembered her as a cheery little flirt whom he had met during the previous season; and finding her companionable and amusing, determined to carry on a flirtation which should serve as a pastime, and, at the break-up of the party, be consigned to that limbo already replete with similar *amourettes*. The presence of Captain Lyster, and the unmistakable evidence of his passion for the young lady, gave Mr. Beresford very little annoyance; he had a notion that, save in very exceptional cases, of which indeed he had had no experience, women had a horror of an earnest lover; that watchings and waitings, hangings on words, deep gazings into eyes, and all outward signs of that passion which induces melancholy and affords themes for poets, were as much *rococo* and out of date, as carrying a lady's glove in your hat and perpetually seeking a fight with some one on her account. He thought that women hated "dreary" lovers, and were far more likely to be won by rattle, laughter, and raillery than by the deepest devotion of a silent and sighing order. Moreover, as he was only going in for flirtation, he would make his running while it lasted, and leave the captain to come in with the weight-carrying proprieties after he had gone.

So far at first. Then came the recollection of

his straightened position, the reflection that Miss
Townshend was an heiress, and the determination
to go in seriously for a proposal—a determination
which was very short-lived, owing to the discovery
of the lady's engagement to Gustav Schröder.
From the time of her marriage, Mrs. Schröder
was by Beresford mentally relegated to a corps
which included several married ladies of his acquaintance; for the most part young and pretty
women, whose husbands were either elderly, or
immersed in business, or, what was equally available, immersed in pleasure, and more attentive to
other men's wives than to their own; ladies who
required "notice," as they phrased it, and who
were sufficiently good-looking to command it from
some men, between whom and themselves there
existed a certain understanding. Nothing criminal
nor approaching to criminality; for despite the
revelations of the Divorce Court, there is, I take
it, a something, whether it be in what is called
our phlegmatic temperament, whether it be in the
bringing-up of our English girls,—bringing-up of
domesticity utterly unknown to Continental-bred

young ladies, which hallows and keeps constantly present the image of the doting father and the tender mother, and all the sacred home-associations,—a something which strengthens the weak and arrests the hand of the spoiler, and leaves the sacrifice incomplete. The necessity for "notice," or for "being understood," or "for having some one to rely on" (the husband engaged in business or in the House being, of course, utterly untrustworthy), has created a kind of society which I can only describe as a kind of solid bread-and-butter *demi-monde*—a *demi-monde* which, as compared with that state of existence known in France under the title, is as a club to a tavern, where the same things are carried on, but in a far more genteel and decorous manner. The relations of its different members to each other are as free from Wertherian sentimentalism as they are from Parisian license, and would probably be considered severely correct by that circle of upper Bohemians, of whose lives the younger Dumas has constituted himself the chronicler.

Having, then, mentally appointed Mrs. Schröder a member of this society, Mr. Beresford took upon himself the office of her cavalier, and behaved to her in due form.   When they were in company together, he sedulously kept his eyes upon her, strove to anticipate her wishes, and let her see that it was she who entirely absorbed him; he always dropped his voice when he spoke to her, even though it were about the merest trifle; and he invariably took notice of the arrangements of her dress, hair, and appearance in general, and made suggestions which, being in excellent taste, were generally approved and carried out.   Then he found out Mrs. Schröder's romantic side, a little bit of nineteenth-century sentiment, dashed with drawing-room cynicism, which found its exponent in Mr. Owen Meredith's weaker verses; and there they found plenty of quotations about not being understood, and the " little look across the crowd," and " what is not, might have been," and other choice little sentiments which did not tend to elevate Mr. Gustav Schröder, then hard at work in the City, in his wife's good opinion. Indeed, being a very weak little woman, with a parasitical tendency to cling for support to something, and being without that something, which she had hitherto found in Barbara, free from the dread which her father's presence always imposed upon her, and having no companion in her husband, Mrs. Schröder began to look forward with more and more eagerness to her opportunities of meeting Charles Beresford, to take greater and greater delight in his attentions and his conversation, and to substitute a growing repugnance for her hitherto passive endurance of Mr. Schröder. Charles Beresford was gradually coming to occupy the principal position in her thoughts, and this that gentleman perceived with mingled feelings of gratified vanity and annoyance. "She's going a little too fast!" he had said to himself; "this sort of thing is all very well; but she's making it a mile too palpable! People will talk, and I'm not in a position to stand any public scandal; and as for bolting, or any thing of that sort, by Jove, it would be sheer ruin and nothing less." In this frame of mind, it had more than once occurred to Mr. Beresford to speak to Mrs. Schröder, and caution her as to her bearing towards him; but fortunately for him, so thoroughly void of offence had been all their relations hitherto, that he scarcely dared to hint at what he intended to convey, without risking the accusation of imputing evil by his very advice. And in the mean time, while he hesitated what course to take, came Dr. Prater's information, which at once changed all his plans.

The day after the conversation at the Flyby-nights, Mr. Beresford left town and remained away for a week. The first day after his return, he went into Mr. Simnel's room at the Office, and found that gentleman as usual surrounded with work. Contrary, however, to his general custom, Simnel no sooner looked up and saw Beresford than he threw down the pen which he was ply-ing, rose, and advancing shook his friend heartily by the hand.

"Glad to see you back, Charley!" he said; "I was afraid you were off for a ramble by your leaving no message and no address. Some of the old games, eh? You must give them up now,

Master Charley, and live circumspectly; by Jove, you must."

"Nothing of the sort," replied Beresford. "Gayford, who was chief here before Maddox, was an old friend of our family; and he's ill, poor old boy, so I went out of charity to stay with him. He's got a place at Berkhampstead, and there's deuced good hunting-country round there. I had three capital days; Gayford's daughters were out; clipping riders, those girls! good as Kate Mellon any day!"

"Indeed!" said Mr. Simnel, wincing a little at the 'name: "I should think flirting with any body's daughters, be they ever so 'clipping,' as you call it, would be time wasted for you just now, wouldn't it?"

"What do you mean?" asked Beresford, knowing perfectly, but anxious that the declaration should come from his companion.

"Mean!" said Simnel, somewhat savagely. "What am I likely to mean? That you ought to stick to your duties here and earn your salary; that Sir Hickory has heard that you go to the

Argyle Rooms, and is going to speak to Lord Palmerston about it; that you're hurting your health or spoiling your complexion by keeping late hours,—is that why I'm likely to tell you to live circumspectly? What rubbish it is fencing with me in this way! You know that the last time we met was at that night-club of yours; that we had a talk there with Dr. Prater; and that you determined—"

"I know," interrupted Beresford with a start —"I know," he continued, looking round, "I'm not over particular; but I confess this plotting for a dead man's shoes seems to me infernal rascality."

"What do you mean by 'plotting,' Charles Beresford? *I* am plotting for no dead man's shoes. *I* have no hope of marrying a pretty widow, and having a splendid income; and as for rascality—"

"There, I didn't mean it; I only thought—"

"Nor, on the other hand," pursued Mr. Simnel, relentlessly, "am *I* over head and ears in debt, pressed by Jews, horribly impecunious, and—"

"Leave me alone, Simnel, can't you? I

know all this; and as you must be perfectly certain, I've turned this Schröder affair over in my mind a hundred times already."

"And what have you decided?"

"To go in for it at all hazards."

"I think you're right," said Simnel quietly; "it seems to me your last chance; and though it's not strictly a very nice business, there are hundreds of men holding their heads up before the world, which very much esteems them, who have made their money in far worse transactions. You'll require an immense amount of patience and tact."

"The former undoubtedly. Prater said he might go at any moment if—what was it?—anything excited or annoyed him. Question is what does excite a fellow of that sort—Muscovadoes being high, or gray-shirtings scarce, or pig-iron in demand, or some of those things one sees in the paper—banks breaking or stocks falling, eh? As for the tact, I don't think that will be required now."

"How do you mean—*now*?"

" Because it's all squared already," said Beresford complacently. " I've only to go in and win whenever I like, I imagine. To tell the truth—though a man doesn't talk of these things, of course—I've been fighting shy of it lately, rather than pressing it on."

" Yes, yes, of course," said Simnel impatiently; " I know all about that but don't you see that the greatest tact will be required because your plan of operations must be entirely changed ? You have been carrying on a very animated flirtation within certain limits; but now you are going in for a totally different thing. You are going in—sit down, and let us talk this over quietly, it's rather important; I know you've great experience in such matters; but just listen to my humble advice, it may be worth hearing,—you are going in to make sure of marrying a woman after her husband's death; an event likely to occur at any time. To insure success there are two ways—one by compromising her—"

" By Jove, Simnel!" exclaimed Beresford through his shut teeth.

"Be quiet, and don't interrupt—I'm not going to brush the down off your virtue! As I said, by compromising her, by which you gain a hold upon her which she cannot shake off, and must always acknowledge and bow to, when required. But this, besides being wrong and unjust, and all that sort of thing—which I don't so much mind—is risky, which I dislike; and if detected, brings the whole fabric to the ground. So we may put that on one side."

"Ah!" said Beresford, with a sigh of relief; "and the other?"

"The other is a totally different method, and unlike any thing you have ever tried, I suspect, with any one. It is simply by professing hopeless, unswerving, unconquerable spooniness. You have hitherto—pardon the question—merely looked and sighed, &c.? Ah, I thought so; that gesture was quite satisfactory as to the amount of tenderness. Well now, then, you must declare yourself. Quietly, of course, and, if you please, without any manifestations, which would entirely spoil our plan, the essence whereof is virtue. You

declare yourself to this effect: that you are so
completely smitten that you can keep silence
no longer; that previous to going away for a
lengthened period (for you believe that expatria-
tion is the only thing that will afford temporary
relief), you have determined on speaking to her,
fearing she might think your absence strange,
or hear it's cause wrongly explained by somebody
else; that yours is not like the feeble sentiment
of the butterflies who flutter around her, &c., &c.;
but a deep and stedfast passion, which will only
cease with life.   You know all that business.
Then, that your respect for her is so great, that
you will not give scandal the smallest chance of
a whisper.   Had you met in happier times—oh!
you did, eh?   Well, then, had you been in a
position, when you first met, to have offered, &c. ;
but now, too late! love for ever; but leave for
ever—foreign climes."

"Yes; but you know well enough I can't go
abroad, and—"

"My dear fellow, she'll never dream of your
doing any thing of the sort.   If I've any know-

ledge of women, she'll be deeply affected, as she ought to be, by your deucedly romantic story. She'll say a good deal about ' if," in reference to former years; she'll state her full determination to do nothing approaching the smallest shadow of wrong; but she'll avow she should be miserable at the idea of being the cause of your banishment, and therefore she'll entreat you to stop in England and be her brother."

" Be her brother?"

" Ay, and a first-rate position you'll have of it as her brother. There'll be an immense amount of sentiment in the connexion; she'll defer to you in every thing; your presence will always keep every body else off, and she'll never dream of carrying on with any one but you. How could she expect again to meet with such delicacy as you've shown? And, if any thing *should* happen, you're safe to be first in the field and to carry off the cup. Now do you see the line of country?"

" Oh, yes, I see it fast enough, and I've no doubt I can manage it. It's rather a duffing business altogether; however, needs must, and I mustn't risk any more flukes. One thing I *am* curious about, Simnel."

" What's that ?"

" Why *you* take such an interest in this business? You first put me on to it, and you've evidently given it some of your precious time in thinking it out while I've been away. Be frank for once in your life, and say—"

" Why does it interest *me*?" said Simnel, nursing his leg, and giving a grin which showed all his big teeth. " Well, Master Charley, your memory has never been good, but you might occasionally recollect that you owe me eight hundred pounds!"

" Yes," said Beresford, " I know that well enough; but it isn't for that alone. You'll be safe to get that, if I marry and come into money; but there's something more in it than that, I know. It's that business with the name of that firm that you made me say to old Townshend, isn't it now, eh ?"

" What, Pigott and Wells!" said Simnel, rocking to and fro—" Pigott and Wells of Combcardingham? Well, perhaps that has some thing to do with it; who knows? Meantime, stick to what I've told you; begin at once, and in a month's time come to me with a good report."

And so ended the colloquy between this precious pair.

Pursuing his instructions with a certain amount of relish, and all the experience of an accomplished and versatile actor, Mr. Beresford threw himself into his new character with spirit, and made a decided hit in it. All the raillery and nonsense, all the smiles and laughter, had vanished. Owen Meredith had been exchanged for Lord Byron; and Mr. Beresford as a nineteenth-century London-made Giaour was doing terrible execution to that feeble little bit of Mrs. Schröder's anatomy which she called her heart. There was no one to say a kind word, to give proper advice, to the poor little woman in her need. Barbara was absolutely lost to her: she had been two or three times to Great Adullam Street, and Barbara had returned the call; but there was evident restraint on both sides. The outside show of friendship

remained, but there was no animating spirit;
none such, at least, as to call for the kind of
confidence which Alice Schröder would gladly
have made, had she received the slightest invita-
tation. But Barbara was not the Barbara of old
days: she looked worn and anxious, was constantly preoccupied, and answered at random; she
confined herself, moreover, to the merest com-
monplaces in her conversation, so that Alice got
no help from her. Nor from her father had she
any supervision: strict to a fault before her marriage, Mr. Townshend, having once settled his
daughter, imagined that his duty in life was
done, and that henceforth he might devote himself entirely to pleasure, consisting in haunting the
City by day and the whist-tables at the Travellers
by night. And it began to be noticed that this
hitherto model British merchant drank a great
deal of wine with his dinner, and a great deal of
brandy after it; and there were ugly rumours
running about 'Change and drifting through Gar-
raway's; and Townshend's clerks were rather in
request at the Bay Tree, and were manifestly

pumped as to whether there was any thing wrong
with their governor, under the guise of being requested to "put a name" to what they would like
to drink. It may be imagined, therefore, that
under this state of circumstances Mr. Townshend
had neither time nor inclination to bestow any
advice upon that daughter, who, as he was in
the habit of saying, "had made such a splendid
alliance." With her husband Alice had, as has
before been said, nothing in common. He was
a cold, proud, well-meaning man, who gloried as
much as a white-blooded elderly person can be
said to glory in his riches and his state, and who
liked to have a pretty, elegant, well-dressed woman
before him at table, in the same way that he liked
to have a stout big-whiskered butler in a white
waistcoat behind him. He liked his wife, when he
had time to think about her; but he had been
brought up in business, and that absorbed his
whole attention by day; while giving or going
to parties, in which he could spend the result of
what he had attained by business, occupied him
at night. But he had the highest opinion of Mrs.

Schröder's conduct, which he imagined was on a par with every thing else in the establishment—real and genuine; and he paid her bills, and presented her with cheques, with lavish generosity. Only he was not exactly the man on whose bosom a wife could lay her head and confess that she was tempted beyond her strength.

There was a man who, without being much mixed up with this little episode in the great drama of human life, overlooked some of the scenes, and saw the dangers to which one of the characters was rapidly exposing herself. That man was Fred Lyster, the one sentiment of whose life—his love for Alice Townshend—was as fresh and as green and as pure as ever. The announcement of her engagement was a great shock to him, and he had taken care only to meet her face to face once or twice since her marriage. The meeting upset him; and though she was apparently unconscious of any feeling in the matter, it did her no good; and there was no earthly reason why it should be. But he went every where where she went, and watched her in the distance; his ears were always on the alert whenever her name was mentioned in club smoke-rooms and such-like haunts of gossip; and he found, as he had dreaded with fatal prescience, at Bissett, that Beresford was on the trail. Long and earnestly he deliberated with himself as to what course he should pursue. Should he pick a quarrel on some other topic with Beresford, and shoot him? Shooting had gone out of fashion; and if he killed his man, he should be exiled from England; if he didn't kill him, where was the use of challenging him? Should he speak to Mr. Townshend? or was there no female friend to whom he could apply? Yes; Barbara Churchill. In Barbara Churchill he had the greatest confidence, and to her he would go at once.

CHAPTER VIII.

BARBARA'S FIRST LESSON IN THE MANEGE.

FOR some few months after the events just described, the lives of those who form the characters of this little drama passed evenly on without the occurrence of any circumstance worthy of special record on the part of their historian. Mr. Beresford, implicitly following Mr. Simnel's advice, proceeded to lay siege to Mrs. Schröder in the manner agreed upon, and found his advances received very much after the fashion predicted by his astute friend. In all child-like simplicity Mrs. Schröder firmly believed in the baneful influence which she had unconsciously exercised over her admirer, and strove to make him amends by a charitable and sentimental pity. She could perfectly appreciate all his feelings; for was not she herself misunderstood? had her girlhood's dream been realised? what was wealth, what was position, to her? was she not mated with one who, &c.? So she not merely permitted but encouraged Mr. Beresford's fraternal sentiments; though she by no means eschewed the world and its frivolity, and gave herself up to solitary romance. On the contrary, she went out a great deal into society, and had frequent receptions at home; Beresford being her constant but always unobtrusive companion. It is difficult to say what motive about this time prompted a considerable change in Mr. Schröder's manner towards his wife; but some such change undoubtedly took place. It may possibly have been that the insufficiency of money as a source of happiness may have dawned upon him, steeped as he was to his very lips in constantly-increasing wealth. It may have been that he suddenly awoke to the fact that he was expected to lavish something more than generosity on the young girl whom he had made the head of his house, and who, as he thought, conducted herself with so much propriety. This new feeling may have had its germ one night when they were sitting in their grand-tier box at the Italian Opera, during the performance of *Der Freischütz;* and as the old familiar strains rang through the house, Gustav Schröder's memory travelled back for five-and-thirty years, and he saw himself a lad of seventeen, seated in the pit of a little German theatre by the side of a plump little girl, who wore a silver arrow through the great knot of her flaxen hair, and down whose cheeks tears were rolling as she listened to the recital of Agatha's woes. He had loved that plump little Kätchen, loved her with a boy's pure and ardent passion; and when sent to his uncle's counting-house in Frankfort, they had parted with bitter tears, and with the exchange of very cheap and worthless love-tokens. He wondered what had become of that five-groschen piece with the hole drilled through it, and the bit of red ribbon. He wondered why he had never loved since those days. And then he looked up and saw his pretty, elegant little wife, whom every one admired and praised; and it flashed upon him that he had never tried to break through the outer crust of

staid formality with which business and the world
had covered him; and he determined to try to
love and be loved once more. And so Mrs.
Schröder, beginning to be dreadfully frightened
at the incantation scene, was astonished to find
her hand gently taken in her husband's, and on
looking up to find his eyes fixed on hers. From
that time out Gustav Schröder was a changed
man; he took frequent holidays from business;
he strove in every way to let his wife see how
anxious he was for her happiness; and she saw it,
and was to a certain extent touched by his conduct. It needed all Mr. Beresford's sophistry,
all his attention and quotation, the employment
of all the art in which he had been indoctrinated
by his friend Simnel, to make head against the
influence which Gustav Schröder's quiet watchful-
ness and fatherly affection were attaining; for the
affection was, after all, more fatherly than con-
jugal in its display. Mr. Schröder was far too
much a man of the world to affect to ignore
his age or the result of his life-habits; and
no one was better pleased than he to see his

wife happy among younger and livelier companions.

A happy influence properly exercised at this time would have been immediately beneficial to Alice Schröder, and have brought matters back into the right course. For instance, ten minutes' talk with Barbara Churchill would have settled the question; for Barbara was to Alice that one grand idol whom we all of us (although we change them at different periods of our lives) set up and worship. And Barbara had not derogated one whit from her high position in Alice's estimation by her marriage. It was exactly the thing that she imagined a girl of her friend's high spirit would do, if pressed to it; there was something romantic in it, savouring of the legends of the high dames of old, who gave themselves to poets after scorning kings; and the whole process entirely agreed with certain of the *dicta* of Mr. Owen Meredith, who, as has been explained, was poet-laureate at the Schröder court. And Alice called on Barbara, and petted her and praised her, and in her silly little way did every thing possible to prevent the smallest *rapproche-ment* between them.   And then Alice went away, and cried in the carriage on her way home, and declared that Barbara was cruel and unkind and unjust, and had utterly changed in every thing.

Were these assertions correct? I fear that at all events they had a certain proportion of truth.   The spirit which had induced Barbara Lexden to marry a man without money, and of, as her friends thought, inferior position; which had made her scorn the threats of being cast off by those among whom her life had hitherto been placed, and to hold to one whom she knew but little, yet trusted much,—this same spirit made her brave the fate to which she had resigned herself, and determined that if she repined, it should be in secret and unheard.   It *was* a mis-take; *that* she had already confessed to herself with bitter tears many and many a time; done in haste, repented at leisure—the old, old story, the old seductive myth, which will find believers for ever and aye.   How often, brooding in the solitude of her chamber, had she gone over the whole business in her mind, linking bit to bit, and endeavouring to find out where the reality had fallen short of the anticipation!

They were poor. Well! had she not expected poverty; had not Frank told her plainly and honourably of his position before he made any declaration? Yes; but she did not understand poverty exactly as she had found it. She knew that they would not be able to give parties, nor to go to the Opera, nor that kind of thing; but she certainly thought that they would go out sometimes, and that she should not be stuck at home for ever. Of course the people who gave parties had a great deal of expense; but those who went to them had none; and it was not expected that any newly-married people living in a small way should entertain in return. But then Frank, after positively refusing to go out a third night running, had given way; but had shaken his head, and looked so serious over a glove-bill which he happened to see on her dressing-table, that she threw on her dressing-gown, and bade him go by himself. She did not care

about going out; but if she went, she would be
decent; she had always been considered to have
a reputation for good taste, and nothing on earth
should make her a dowdy now. She would sooner
stay at home always; indeed there was little
enough to go out for, having to be jolted in
those horrible cabs, that crawled along the streets,
with no room for one's dress, and with the cer-
tainty of being covered with dust or straw, or
some dreadful stuff, when you got out; and then
the insolence of the driver!

And her home? It was small, and dull, and
dreary; but had she been led to anticipate any
thing else? No; she supposed not. And yet
she wore herself out in those gaunt dark rooms,
and chafed in her prison like a bird in its cage.
She had always been a bad correspondent, and
since her marriage had scarcely written any letters
at all; but she would sit mooning over the pages
of a novel, or over the stitches of her embroidery,
until book or work would fall from her hand; and
there she would remain, looking intently at nothing,
staring vacantly before her. Frank caused her to

be supplied regularly with a copy of the *Statesman,* and in it she tried to read his articles—an honest attempt in which she dismally failed. Her aunt had been somewhat of a keen politician, and Barbara was sufficiently well informed on the position of English parties to bear her share in a dinner-table dialogue; but foreign affairs principally occupied Frank's pen in the *Statesman;* and after an attempted course of reading about Moldo-Wallachia, Schleswig-Holstein, and the Principalities, including an immense amount of virtuous indignation, the reason for which she did not comprehend, and the object of which she could not make out, poor Barbara gave it up in despair. She was in the habit of glancing occasionally at that portion of the paper in which Mr. Henchman chronicled the doings of the fashionable world, and recorded the names of those present at great entertainments; and sometimes when Barbara would raise her eyes from the paper and look down the hot vista of frowning houses in Great Adullam Street, where dust and straw were blowing in a penetrating cloud, and whence the dismal howling of itinerant hucksters fell upon the ear, she, remembering what part she recently had played among those of whom she had been reading, and contrasting it with her then life, would bite her lip until the blood started, and sob bitterly.

Where was her spirit, do you ask? Has she not been represented as a girl of special spirit and pluck? Did not the early-narrated incidents of her career, her very marriage, prove this? and is it natural that she should break down before petty annoyances such as these? These questions have been asked; and all I can reply is, that I paint according to my lights and to my experience of life; and I believe that there are hundreds of women of spirit who would bear the amputation of a finger with more fortitude than the non-arrival of a bonnet, and who suffer less in separation from those they dearly love than in the necessity for a daily inspection of the bread-pan.

And Frank, what of him? Had Barbara been deceived in him? had she misjudged his heart, his truth, his love? Not one whit; and yet how different he seemed! Throughout his life, Frank

Churchill had acted on impulse, and had generally pulled through with extraordinary success.
We have seen how, in the railway-journey back
to Bissett, he had argued with himself, had persuaded himself into the determination of leaving
the place and flying from temptation, and how on
the impulse of a moment he settled the career of
his life. To say he had repented of that step,
would have been untrue; equally false would it
have been to say that he had not been seriously
disappointed in its result. The great charm of
Barbara Lexden in his eyes had been her dissi-
milarity from other women. In the quiet circles
in which he moved, there was no one kin to her;
she stood out in bold relief among the fussy wives
and meek colourless daughters of his friends, seem-
ing a being of another sphere. And now, strange
to say, this very contrast which had so captivated
him, was his bane. What though the wives were
fussy; they attended to their households with the
utmost regularity, investigating the smallest matters of domestic detail, keeping down expenses
here, making shift there, and having a comfort-

able home ready for their husbands wearied out with their work. What though the daughters were meek and colourless, without a fragment of taste in dress, without a spark of spirit, without one atom of dash; they were ready to strum the piano, or to play endless games of whist or picquet, when called upon, to enjoy thoroughly such little society as they had among themselves, and, in fact, to make themselves generally amiable. "Their girls did not lollop on the sofa and read trashy novels all day long, my dear!" as Mrs. Harding more than once remarked; "they were not aristocrats, and couldn't jabber Italian; but they didn't lie in bed to breakfast, or be always fiddling with their hair, or dressing or undressing themselves twenty times a day. If those were aristocratic manners, the less she had of them the better."

All this talk, and there was much of it perpetually current, reached Frank Churchill's ears through his mother, and if it did not render him actually unhappy, at least dashed his spirits and checked his joys. He would sit for hours pondering over these things, thinking of his past, when he had only himself and his old mother to care for, wondering what would have been his future, supposing he had married one of the daughters of Mesopotamia, and settled down into the snug humdrum life pursued by those colonists. And then sometimes Barbara would break in upon his reverie, and, looking so brilliantly handsome, would come up and kiss his forehead, and say a few loving words untinged by regret or complaint; and he would rejoice in the choice he had made, and thank that fortune which had thrown such a treasure in his way.

There is no doubt that, without in the least degree intending it (indeed, what sacrifice had she not made, would she not make, for her son?), old Mrs. Churchill was a fruitful cause of the petty dissensions which took place between Barbara and her husband. Devoted to Frank, to her natural anxiety for his happiness was superadded an invincible jealousy of the woman who had supplanted his mother in his regard, or at least had pushed her from the highest position therein. Against the actuations of this feeling the old lady strove with all her strength, and made great way; but, like many other intending victors, she imagined the day gained before the enemy had been thoroughly repulsed, and then, neglecting her outposts, laid herself open to an irresistible attack. At first Frank laughed away all these remarks, telling his mother that the difference of age between her and Barbara, the difference of their lives and bringing up, the difference in the style of the present time and the days when Mrs. Churchill lived in the world, caused her to think the young wife's proceedings singular, and her demeanour odd. But *sæpe cadendo*, by constant trituration the old lady's notions got grafted into his brain, and most of the weary self-communings and self-torturings which Frank had, sprung from his mother's unintentional planting.

One day about noon old Mrs. Churchill knocked at the door of Frank's little study, and entering found her son hard at work on an article he was preparing for a review. The old lady seemed in great spirits, kissed her son most affectionately, and said: "Busy as ever, Frank my darling?

As I often used to say, you'll grow to your desk one day, you stick at it so—at least you used to when I lived with you; I don't know much of what you do now;" and she gave a little sigh, made doubly apparent by an attempt to stifle it, as she sat down.

"Why, mum, what nonsense!" said Frank; "you see as much of me as any body now—as much as Barbara, at all events."

"Oh, by the way, how is Barbara?"

"Well, not very brilliant this morning; she's got one of her headaches, and I persuaded her to breakfast in bed."

"Ah, she didn't take much persuading, I fancy. The young girls nowadays are very different from what I remember them; but she'd be tired, poor child, waiting up for you last night."

"She did no such thing, I'm delighted to say," said Frank, smiling, "as I had to write upon the result of the debate, and didn't get home until nearly three o'clock. Poor Barbara was sound asleep at that time, and had been so for some hours."

"Ah, ever since her visitor went away, I suppose?"

"Her visitor? What visitor?"

"Didn't she tell you? How odd! I called in last evening for a volume of *Blunt on the Pentateuch*, and found Captain Lyster here chatting. How odd that Barbara didn't mention it!"

"She was too sleepy both last night and this morning, I imagine," said Frank; "she has frequently told me of his visits."

"Oh, yes, he calls here very often."

"He's a very pleasant fellow," said Frank.

"Is he?" said the old lady, in rather acrid tones. "I didn't think you knew him."

"Not know him!" exclaimed Frank; "why, mother dear, how on earth should he call here if I didn't know him?"

"He might be a friend of your wife's, my dear."

"But my wife's friends are mine, are they not?"

"It does not always follow, Frank," said the old lady calmly; "besides, I thought if he had been a friend of yours he would have called *some-times* when you were at home."

Frank looked up quickly with a flushed face; then said, " What nonsense, mum! the man is an old friend of Barbara's, and comes at such times as are most convenient to himself. You don't understand the set of people he lives with, mum."

".Very likely not, my dear; and I'm sure I'm not sorry for it; for they seem strange enough; at least to a quiet old-fashioned body like myself, who was taught never to receive male friends when my husband—however, that's neither here nor there." And Mrs. Churchill bustled out.

When Barbara came down to luncheon, Frank said to her, " I hear you had Captain Lyster here last night, Barbara."

" Oh, yes," she replied, " I forgot to tell you; he sat here some time."

" He comes pretty frequently, doesn't he ?"

" I don't know," said Barbara, looking up; " I never counted the number of times; you always hear when he has been."

"I wish you'd do something for me, Barbara," said Frank.

"Well, what is it?"

"Just tell Lyster it would be better if he could contrive to call when I'm at home."

"Why?" asked Barbara pointedly.

"Why—well—upon my word—I scarcely know why—except that people talk, you know; and it's better—eh? don't you think?" stammered Frank. He had acted on impulse again, and felt confoundedly ashamed of himself.

"I distinctly decline to do any thing of the sort. I wonder, Frank, you're not ashamed to propose such a thing to me; but I can see what influence has been at work."

"There has been no influence at all; only I choose—"

"And *I* choose that you should find a fitter person than your wife to deliver insulting messages to your friends!"

"Barbara, suppose I were to insist upon your not receiving this man again?"

"You had better not, Frank," said she, moving

towards the door; "you don't know whom you have to deal with." And she swept out of the room.

And this was Barbara's first lesson in the *manège.*

CHAPTER IX.

A GARDEN-PARTY AT UPLANDS.

ALTHOUGH it was only in the first days of July, it had become thoroughly evident that the London season was on the wane. After a lengthened period of inaction, there had been a fierce parliamentary struggle brought about by that rising young gladiator Mr. Hope Ennythink, who had impeached the Prime Minister, brought the gravest charges against the Foreign Secretary, accused the Chancellor of the Exchequer of crass ignorance, and riddled with ridicule the incompetence of the First Lord of the Admiralty. As Mr. Hope Ennythink spoke with a certain amount of cleverness and a great amount of brass, as he was thoroughly up in all the facts which he adduced,—having devoted his life to the study of Hansard, and being a walking edition of that popular work,—and as he was warmly supported by the Opposition, whose great leaders thought highly of the young man, he ran the Government very hard, and gave the Treasury-whips a great deal of trouble to secure even the slight majority which pulled them through. But immediately the fight was over, it was evident that the session was on the point of closing. There was no more excitement; it was very hot weather; and the session and the season were simultaneously doomed. However, the wives and daughters of the members were determined to die hard; there would be at least a fortnight before the prorogation of Parliament, and during that fortnight dinners, balls, fêtes, and opera-visitings were carried on with redoubled activity. To a good many, condemned to autumnal pinchings and scrapings in a dull country-house, it was the last taste of pleasure until next spring.

Upon the gentlemen attached to the room No. 120, in the Tin-Tax Office, the general state of affairs was not without its effect. Mr. Kinchenton was away for his holiday—he generally chose July as the best month for little Percy's sea-bathing—and he rung the changes between Worthing, Bognor, and Littlehampton, in one of which places he would be found in an entire suit of shepherd's-plaid, and always with a telescope slung round him. Mr. Dibb, his liver in a worse state than ever with the hot weather, had felt himself compelled to quit the pleasant environs of Clapton, where he ordinarily resided, and had taken a bed-room at Windmill-Hill, Gravesend, whence he came up to his office every morning, having immediately established sworn animosity with every guard and regular passenger on the North-Kent Railway, and having regular hand-to-hand combats with the man who sat opposite to him, as to whether the window should be up or down—combats commencing at Gravesend and finishing at New Cross. Upon Mr. Boppy had come a new phase of existence, he having persuaded Mrs. Boppy, for the first time since their marriage, to go on a visit to some country friends, thus leaving him his own master *pro tem*. And Mr. Boppy availed himself of this opportunity to give a bachelor-party, cards and supper, at which Mr. Pringle was the master of the revels, and they all enjoyed themselves very much, and talked about it afterwards to Mr. Boppy; little thinking of the unrevealed misery that wretched convivialist was enduring on account of his being unable to rid the window-curtains of the smell of tobacco-smoke, by which Mrs. B. would learn of the past symposium, and would "warm" her husband accordingly. Mr. Prescott and Mr. Pringle had been going on much the same as usual; and Mr. Crump never went out of town because his pay was stopped when he was absent from his office, and he never had any friends who wished to see him.

It was a very hot morning, the sun blazed in through the windows of No. 120, and upon the head of Mr. Pringle, who was copying items of account on to a large ruled sheet of paper.

"Item, every horse for draught or burden—item, each dog, sheep, swine—I'll be blowed if I'll do any more of it," said Mr. Pringle, casting down his pen and rubbing his head. "I must have some soda-water! Prescott, James, was there too much lemon in Quartermaine's punch last night, or was it that the whitebait are growing too large to be wholesome? Something was wrong, I know! Crump, my boy, you're nearest the cellar; just hand me a bottle of the corrective."

Mr. Crump certainly was nearest the cellar, which was in fact the cupboard which should have been his property, but which had been appropriated by Messrs. Pringle and Prescott as a soda-water store.

"That's a good fellow; now you're up, would you mind just handing me a bit of ice out of the basin? Thanks! What a good Crumpy it is! What's the matter, Mr. Dibb?"

"Can't you be silent for an instant, Mr. Pringle? You are perpetually gabbling. Can't you let us have a moment's peace?"

"I can generally," said Mr. Pringle, with an affectation of great frankness; "but, somehow, not this morning. I seem to be inspired

by this delicious fluid. I think I shall write a
book called Songs of Soda-water, or Lays of
the Morning after. That wouldn't be a bad
title, would it, Dibb?"

Mr. Dibb took no notice of this, beyond glaring
at Mr. Boppy, who had laughed; and there was
silence for a few minutes, broken by Mr. Prescott,
who said, " When do you go on leave, George ?"

" In September, sir," replied Pringle. " That's
the genial month when the leaves come off."

" Where are you going ?"

" That depends upon how much tin I've got.
It strikes me, from the present look-out, that the
foreign watering-place of Holloway is about as far
as I shall be able to get. There's a tightness in
the money-market that's most infernal."

" Why don't you apply to your godfather,
old Townshend? He's always treated you with
kindness."

" Yes; with un-remitting kindness! wouldn't
send me a fiver to save me from gaol. Oh, no !
I'll manage somehow. When are you going ?"

" Well, I wanted a few days in September

myself, if I could get away. I've some shooting offered me at Murray's."

" Murray's?   Oh, ah! the parent of that nice little girl! je twig.   And the Paterfamilias is a jolly old bird, isn't he, and likes his drink, and has plenty of money? in which case pater-familiarity does not breed contempt."

"They are old friends of my people you know; and the old gentleman's been very civil to me."

"Ah! and the young lady hasn't been rude, has she?—at least I judged not, from what I saw. She rides deuced well; but what a long time she takes to mount! and when you had swung her to the saddle, I noticed that her reins took an immense deal of arranging!"

"Don't be an idiot, George! you're always fancying things."

"And you're always fancying girls, and my life's passed in keeping you out of scrapes."

" By the way, do you ever see any thing of—"

"Of *the other?* Ah, base deceiver! fickle as the wind, or the what's his name! Yes, I've met poor Kitty once or twice, and, without any nonsense, she looked thoroughly seedy and worn."

"Poor dear Kitty, I'm so sorry! I—"

"Oh, yes, we know all about it; 'he loves and he rides away,' and all the rest of it. But, joking apart, Master Jim, it's a very good thing that business is over. I was really afraid at one time you were going to grief. But—hollo! for me?" These last words thrown off at a tangent to a messenger who entered the room with a letter.

"No, sir; for Mr. Prescott."

"Ah! I don't like letters generally; but that's not a blue one, and looks tolerably healthy. What's it about, George?"

"Read for yourself;" and Mr. Prescott tossed the letter over to him.

"Mrs. Schröder—garden-fête—Uplands," said Pringle, reading. "Oh, ah! I knew all about that, but I didn't mention it, because I wasn't sure that you'd be asked; and as a certing persing is going, you'd have been as mad as a hatter at losing the chance of meeting her."

"What's Uplands?" asked Prescott.

"Uplands is no end of a jolly place which Schröder has taken for the summer and autumn. He has got some tremendous operation in the mines, or the funds, or some of those things that those City fellows get so brutally rich with; and he must be in town two or three times a week. So instead of going to Switzerland, as he intended, he has rented Uplands, which is about seven miles from town, and might be seventy. Out north way, through Whittington; stunning Italian villa, fitted up no end, with conservatories, and big grounds, and a lake, and all sorts of fun. Belonged to another City buffer, who's over-speculated himself and gone to Boulogne. That *is* a comfort; they do go to smash sometimes; but even then they've generally settled as much as the Chief Commissioner's income on their wives. Schröder heard of this; pounced upon it at once; and this is to be Mrs. Schröder's first garden-party."

"I'm very glad I'm asked, if—"

"Glad you're asked! I should think so; it'll be a first-rate party. There'll be no shy ices or

Cape cup; Gunter does the commissariat; the
Foreign Office has been instructed to send a lot
of eligible Counts; and Edgington will supply the
marquee."

"I was going to say, when you were kind
enough to interrupt me, that I'm glad I'm asked,
if Miss Murray is to be there."

"She'll be there, sir, fast enough; and you
shall devote yourself to her, and be the Murray's
Guide; and I'll be your courier, and go before
you to see that all is square. I mean to enjoy
myself that day, and no mistake."

"This is the place, Jim!" said Mr. Pringle, as
on the day of the party they drove in a hansom
along a meadow-bordered road some two miles the
country side of the little village of Whittington.
"That's the house, that white building with the
high tower; no end of a smoke-room that tower
makes! it's fitted up with lounges and Indian mat-
ting; all the windows hook outwards, and there's
a view all over every where! What a lot of traps,
too!—like the outside of the Star and Garter on

a Sunday afternoon.. That's the Guards' drag,
I suppose; I know there was a lot of them
coming down—"

" And there's old Murray's carriage; I'd know
that any where," interrupted Prescott.

" Is it? well, then, you'll be all right. Easy,
cabby; we don't want to be thrown into the very
midst of the aristocracy; we'll get out here, and
walk quietly up."

Mr. Pringle had by no means given an exag-
gerated description of the beauties of Uplands.
The house stood on the brow of the hill, under
which nestled the little village of Whittington,
the only cluster of buildings within a couple of
miles' range. All round it lay large meadows,
through which flowed, in tiny silver thread, the
river Brent; while far away on the horizon lay
a thick heavy cloud betokening the position of
Babylon the Great. In the house the rooms,
though somewhat low, were large and cheerful,
and the grounds were laid out in every variety
of exquisite taste. There were broad lawns,
whereon the croquet-players loved to linger; and

noble terraces, where the elderly people sat, sheltered alike from the sun and the wind; and dark winding shady walks, down which, at the close of evening, couples would be seen stealing, and being questioned on their return, would declare that they had been to see the syringa,—a statement which was invariably received with derision, or, as the poet hath it, " Doubts would be muttered around, and the name be suggested of Walker." And there was a large lake with a real Venetian gondola upon it, very black and gloomy, and thoroughly realising the notion of a " coffin clapt in a canoe," and a large light shallop with an awning, and a couple of outriggers and a water-quintain for those people who preferred athletics to ease, and sunstrokes to comfort.

"This is the right sort of thing, isn't it, my boy?" said Mr. Pringle, as they passed along. " I suppose you could put up with a crib like this, couldn't you? What a lot of people! every body in London here! How do, doctor? Dr. Prater, very good little party; took me behind the scenes at the Opera once, and gave me a certificate when

I wanted sick-leave. See that tall man in the fluffy white hat? Mincing-Lane fellow merchant; named Hill; capital fellow, but drops his *h's* awfully. They call him the *Malade Imaginaire*, because he calls himself 'ill when he isn't. That's his wife in the black dress with white spots on it, like change for a sovereign. Those two tall fellows are in the Second Life-Guards. Look at the nearest one to us, that's Punch Croker; don't he look like an ape? I always long to give him a nut: the other man's Charley Greville, a very good fellow; they tell a capital story about him. His uncle was a tremendous old screw, who left Charley his heir. When the will was read, the first clause contained the expression of a hope that his debts would not be paid. Charley had a copy of this clause sent round to all the creditors, with an indorsement that he, as executor, would religiously fulfil the desire of the deceased. There was a terrible scrimmage about it, and the lawyers are at it now, I believe."

"Isn't this our man—Beresford?"

" Of course it is, and there's Mr. Schröder close
by him.   We'll go up and make our salaams."

So the young men wound through the crowd,
and were very cordially received by Mrs. Schröder,
and indeed by Mr. Beresford.   For the Commissioner knew his popularity in the Office and was
pleased at it, and was always glad to meet decent-
looking men belonging to it in society.   "It improved the tone of the confounded place," he used
to say.   Talking to Mrs. Schröder was Mr. Sergeant Shivers, one of the ornaments of the Old
Bailey bar; a tremendously eloquent man in the
florid and ornate style, with a power of cross-ex-
amination calculated to turn a witness inside out,
and a power of address able to frighten the jury
into fits; but who scorned all these advantages,
and was never so happy as when talking of and
to great people.   He was on his favourite topic
when Prescott and Pringle arrived.

" Ah, my dear Mrs. Schröder," he was saying,
" isn't it sad? The duchess herself sent for me, and
said, ' Now, Mr. Sergeant, speak to him yourself.
You have experience of life; above all, you have

experience of our order. Tell Philip what will be the result of this marriage with Lady Di!' I promised her grace I would; and I did. I spoke not only to Lord Philip, but to Lord Ronald and Lord Alberic, his brothers. But it was no good; the marriage has come off, and now the poor duchess is in despair. Ah! there's Lady Nettleford! I must go and condole with her on the affair;" and the learned sergeant bowed himself off.

"Ah! 'Good-by to the bar and its moaning,' as Kingsley says," remarked Mr. Pringle. "What a dreary bird! Now I see you're fidgetting to be off, Jim; and I know perfectly well why; so we'll go and look after the Murray. What a pity she's not got up in red, like her namesakes! then we could recognise her a mile off."

"There she is !" suddenly exclaimed Mr. Prescott. "There! just crossing the end of the croquet-ground. I'm off, George. I shall find you in plenty of time to go together;" and Mr. Prescott strode away in great haste.

"Very good," said Mr. Pringle; "'and she was left lamenting.' I believe I am in the position of the daughter of the Earl of Ullin; if not, why not? There's no fair young form to hang upon me; man delights me not, nor woman either; so I'll see if there's any moselle-cup handy."

Among those present at the Uplands *fête* were Frank Churchill and Barbara. Alice Schröder had made a great point of their coming; and though at first Barbara refused, yet her husband so strongly seconded the invitation, that she at length gave way and consented. It was a trying time for Barbara: she knew she would there be compelled to meet many of the members of that old set amongst which her youth had been passed, and which she had so sedulously avoided since her marriage, and she was doubtful of her reception by them. Not that that would have distressed Barbara one jot; she would have swept past the great Duchess of Merionethshire herself with up-lift eyebrows and extended nostrils; but she knew that Frank was horribly sensitive, and she feared lest any of his sympathies should be jarred. More-over, she felt certain that Captain Lyster would

be at the Uplands; and though since the day of
the little outbreak his name had not been mentioned, and all having been made up with a kiss
had gone smoothly since, Barbara had an inward
dread that the sight of him would arouse Frank's
wrath and lead to mischief. However, they came.
Barbara was very charmingly dressed; and if her
face were a little pale and her expression somewhat
anxious, her eye was as bright and her bearing
as proud as ever. Alice Schröder received her in
the warmest manner, kissed her affectionately, and
immediately afterwards without the slightest intention planted a dagger in her breast, by express-
ing delight at "seeing her among her old friends
again." "These old friends"—*i.e.* persons whom
she had been in the habit of constantly meeting
in society, and who had envied and hated her—
were gathered together in numbers at Uplands,
and all said civil things to Barbara; indeed, the
great Duchess of Merionethshire actually stepped
forward a few paces—a condescension which she
very rarely granted,—and after welcoming Barbara, begged that Mr. Churchill might be pre-

sented to her, "as a gentleman of whom she had heard so much." Barbara rather opened her eyes at this; but after the presentation it was explained by the duchess saying, "My son-in-law, Lord Hailey, has often expressed his recognition of the services rendered to him by your pen, Mr. Churchill." For Lord Hailey was Foreign Secretary at that time, and certainly gave Churchill plenty of opportunities of defending him. And as they moved away, Barbara heard the duchess say, "What a fine-looking man!" and Mr. Sergeant Shivers, who was thoroughly good-natured, began loudly blowing the trumpet of Frank's abilities. So that Barbara was happier than she had been for some time; and her happiness was certainly not decreased by seeing that the cloud had left Frank's brow, and that he looked in every way his former self.

"Now Barbara," said Alice Schröder, approaching them, "we are getting up two new croquet sets, and want members for each. You'll play, of course? I recollect how you used to send me spinning at Bissett—oh, by the way, have you heard? poor dear Sir Marmaduke, so ill at Pau, or somewhere—"

" Ill?   Sir Marmaduke ill?

" Yes, poor dear! isn't it sad?   And Mr. Churchill will play too; but not on the same side.   I can't have you on the same side; you're old married people now; and both such good players too!   Let me see; Captain Lyster, will you take Mrs. Churchill on your side?"

Captain Lyster bowed, shook hands, and expressed his delight.   Frank Churchill shook hands with Lyster; but as he did so, a flush passed over his face.

" Now, then, that set is full," said Mrs. Schröder; " who is the captain of the other set, playing at the other ground? oh, you, Mr. Pringle!   Will you take Mr. Churchill away with you; you only want one, I think?"

" No, madam," said Pringle, with a serio-comic sigh; " I only want one; but I shall want that one all my life.   Come along, Mr. Churchill."   And he and Frank started off to the lower lawn together.

Barbara had always been very fond of croquet. She played well; relying more upon the effectiveness of her aim than the result of her calculations. She had a perfect little foot; and she croqueted her adversaries far away with as much science as malice. She enjoyed the game thoroughly, as, not having played for months, she rejoiced at finding that she retained all her skill; but she could not help perceiving that Captain Lyster was dull and preoccupied, and that he attended so little to the game as to require perpetual reminding when it was his turn to play. Indeed, despite all Barbara's exertions, they might have lost the game—for their opponents were wary and persevering—had it not been for the steady play of their coadjutors, Mr. Prescott and Miss Murray, who evinced a really remarkable talent for keeping close together, and nursing each other through all the difficult hoops. At length they won with flying colours, and were going to begin a new game, when Captain Lyster said, "Mrs. Churchill, I should be so grateful for a few minutes' talk with you on a really important subject. Please, don't play again, but let us stroll." Barbara had all faith in Fred Lyster's truth and honour; she had known him for years, and more than half-suspected the secret of his early attachment to Alice; so that she had no hesitation in saying, " Certainly, Captain Lyster, if you wish it;" then adding with a smile, " You will not miss us much, will you, Mr. Prescott?" she and the Captain strolled away.

Then, as they walked, Fred Lyster talked long and earnestly. He told Barbara that he addressed her as one who, he knew, took the deepest interest in Alice Schröder's welfare; indeed, as one who had been as her sister in times past. He touched lightly on the disparity in age between Alice and her husband, and upon the difference in all their habits, tastes, and opinions; he said that she was thus doubtless driven to her own resources for amusement, and that her utter simplicity and childishness made her the easy prey of designing people. Then, with the utmost delicacy, he went on to point out that for some time Beresford's attentions to Mrs. Schröder had been most marked; that his constant presence at their house, or in attendance on her when she went out, had attracted attention, and that at length it had become common club-gossip. Only on the previous night he had heard that it had been publicly discussed in the smoke-room of the Minerva; that an old gentleman, an old friend of the family, had announced his intention of speaking to Mr. Schröder about it. What was to be done? He (Lyster), deeply pained at it all, had no authority, no influence, no right, to mix himself with the matter. Would not Mrs. Churchill, in pity for her friend, talk seriously with Mrs. Schröder about it? She was all-potential. Mrs. Schröder believed implicitly in her, and would undoubtedly follow her advice. Would not Mrs. Churchill do this, for pity's sake?"

Barbara was very much astonished and very much shocked. She had always known Alice to be weak and vain and silly; she knew that her marriage with Mr. Schröder had been one made solely at her father's instigation; but having lived entirely out of the set for the last few months, she had no idea of the intimacy with Mr. Beresford, whose acquaintance she considered was by no means desirable. She was entirely at a loss what to do, being of opinion that her influence over Alice had all died out. However, if Captain Lyster thought otherwise, and if he counselled and urged her taking such a step, she would not refuse; she would take an early opportunity of seeking an interview with Alice, and giving that silly girl—silly, and nothing more, she was certain—a very serious talking to; "and then, Captain Lyster, let us trust that this horrible gossip will be put a stop to." As Barbara said this, she smiled and put out her hand. Poor Fred bent over it, and when he raised his head to say, "Mrs. Churchill, you will have done an angel's work!" there were tears in his eyes.

Meantime Frank Churchill, with doubt and distrust at his heart, engendered by having to leave Barbara in company with Captain Lyster, went away with Pringlo to the lower croquet-ground, where they and others played a succession of games with varying success, in all of which Frank distinguished himself by ferocious swiping, and Mr. Pringle came to grief in an untimely manner. At length, when they were tired, Frank and Pringle walked away together—the former on the look-out for his wife, the latter listening with great deference to such scraps of his companion's conversation as he was treated with; for Mr. Pringle had a great reverence for "people who write books," and, in common with a great many, looked upon the production of a something printable as an occult art. "It always seems such a rum thing to me," said he ingenuously, "how you first think about it, and then how you put it down! You write leaders, Mr. Churchill, eh? Oh yes, we heard of you at our office, the Tin-Tax, you know! That article in the *Statesman* about old Maddox and his K.C.B.'ship, they all declared it was you."

As Churchill only said "Indeed!" in an absent manner, and was still looking about him,

Pringle proceeded: "Oh, of course you won't let out it was your work—*we* understand that! but it must be jolly to be able to give a fellow one for himself sometimes! a regular bad one, enough to make him drink! I should think that was better fun than novel-writing; though novel-writing must be easier, as you've only got to describe what you see. I think I could do that —this afternoon, for instance, and all the swells and queer people about. The worst of it is, you must touch it up with a bit of love, and I'm not much of a hand at that; but I suppose one could easily see plenty of it to study from. For instance, do you see those two at the end of this walk, under the tree? I suppose that's a spooning match, isn't it? How he is laying down the law! and she gives him her hand, and he bends over it—"

"Damnation!" exclaimed Churchill.

"Hollo!" said Pringle, "what's the matter?"

"Nothing!" said Churchill; "I twisted my foot, that was all!"

Barbara tried several times that evening to meet Frank; but he avoided her; and it was not until they were in the fly, that she had an opportunity of speaking to him.

"Where on earth have you been, Frank, all day? I hunted and hunted for you, but never succeeded in finding you."

He looked up at her : her eyes were sparkling, her cheek flushed; she was thoroughly happy. The escape from Mesopotamia and its dreariness, the return to scenes similar to those which she had been accustomed to, had worked immediate change. She looked so radiantly beautiful that Frank was half-tempted to spare her; but, after a second's pause, he said,

"I walked all over the grounds. I was in the shrubbery close by you when Captain Lyster kissed your hand."

"What!" exclaimed Barbara, with a start. "It is beneath me to repel such a calumny; but to satisfy your absurd doubt, I tell you plainly you were wrong."

"Will you tell me," asked Frank, in a sad

voice, "that he did not walk with you and talk with you apart? Can you deny it?"

"No!" returned Barbara. "He did both walk and talk with me; he had something very special to say to me, and he said it."

"And it was—?"

"I cannot tell you; it was told to me in confidence; it concerns the reputation of a third person, and I cannot mention it, even to you."

"Then, by the Lord, I'll have an end to this!" said Frank, in a sudden access of passion. "Listen here, Barbara; I'll have no captains, nor any one else, coming to repose confidences with which I'm not to be made acquainted, in my wife! I'll have no shrubbery-walks and whisperings with you! Such things may be the fashion in the circles in which you have lived; but I don't hold with them!"

He could have bitten his tongue out the next instant, when Barbara said, in an icy voice, "It may be the fashion in the circles in which *you* have lived to swear at one's wife, and shout at her so that the coachman hears you; but I don't hold with it, nor, what's more, will I permit it!"

She never spoke again until they reached home, when she stepped leisurely out of the carriage, ignoring Frank's proffered arm, and went silently to bed.

CHAPTER X.

SHOWING WHO WERE " PIGOTT AND WELLS."

MR. SIMNEL, the secretary, sat at his desk, hard at work as usual, but evidently tempering the dullness of the official minutes with some recollections of a lively nature, as now and then he would put down his pen, and smile pleasantly, nursing his knee the while. " Yes," he said softly to himself, " I think I'll do it to-day. I've waited long enough; now I'll put Kitty on to the scent, and stand the racket. *Ruat cœlum!* I'll ride quietly up there this afternoon;" and he touched the small hand-bell, with which he summoned his private secretary. In response to this bell,—not the private secretary, who was lunching with a couple of friends and discussing the latest fashionable gossip,—the door was opened by Mr. Pringle, who begged to know his chief's wishes.

"Eh?" said Simnel, raising his head at the strange voice; "oh, Grammont at lunch, I suppose?—how do you do, Mr. Pringle? I want all the letters brought in at once, please; I'm going away early to-day."

"Certainly, sir," said Mr. Pringle, who objected on principle to interviews with great official swells, such interviews being generally connected in his mind with rebukes known as "carpetings." "I'll see about it, sir."

"Thank you, Mr. Pringle. How are all your people? how is Mrs. Schröder? who is your cousin, I think."

"Yes, my cousin. She's all right; but I'm sorry to say my uncle Mr. Townshend is very ill; so ill that he leaves town for the Continent to-night, and is likely to be away some time."

"Dear me! I'm very sorry to hear that."

"Fact, indeed, sir! I was thinking, sir," said Mr. Pringle, who never missed a chance, "that as Mrs. Schröder may perhaps be rather dull to-morrow after her father's gone, I might perhaps have a day's leave of absence to be with her?"

"Certainly; by all means, Mr. Pringle! Now send in the letters, please." And Mr. Pringle retired into the next room, where he indulged in the steps of a comic dance popular with burlesque-actors, and known as a "nigger break-down."

"Going out of town, eh? likely to be abroad some time! very unwell!" said Mr. Simnel, nursing his leg; "then I must alter my arrangements. I'll go and see him at once, and bring that matter to a head. I can deal with Kitty afterwards." And when Mr. Simnel had signed all the letters brought in to him, he unlocked his desk and took out a paper which he placed in his pocket-book; then carefully locking every thing after him, he departed.

In the Strand he called a cab, and was driven to Austin Friars, where he dismounted, and walked up the street until he came to a large door, on the posts of which were inscribed the words, "Townshend and Co." There was no Co., there never had been; Mr. Townshend was the entire concern; he was the first of his name who had been known in the place, and no one knew his origin. He first made his mark in the City as a daring money-broker and speculator; two or three lucky hits established his fame, and he then became cautious, wary, well-informed, and almost invariably successful. The name of Townshend was highly thought of on 'Change; its owner had been invited to a seat in the Bank Direction, and had been consulted by more than one Chancellor of the Exchequer; he had been a member of the Gresham Club, there made acquaintances, who introduced him into the True Blue and the No-Surrender, for Mr. Townshend was intensely Conservative; and by the time his daughter was fit to head his table (his wife had died years since), he had a set of ancestors on his walls in Harley Street dating from warriors who fought at Ramillies and Malplaquet, down to the " civil servant of the Company," who shook the pagoda-tree in the East, and from whom, as Mr. Townshend said, his first start in life was derived. It is doubtful—and immaterial—whether Mr. Simnel knew or not of the non-existence of the Co. He asked for Mr. Townshend, whether Mr. Townshend was in; and he put the question to one of four young gentlemen who were writing at a desk, which, if it must be called by its right name, was a counter. After a great deal of fencing with this youth, who was reading out wild commercial documents, such as " Two two four nine, Lammas and Childs on National of Ireland—note for dis.," and who declined to be interrupted until he had completed his task,—Mr. Simnel at length got his name sent in to Mr. Townshend, and was shown into the great man's presence.

Mr. Townshend was seated at a large desk covered with papers, which were arranged in the most precise and orderly fashion. He was dressed with great precision, in a blue body-coat and a buff waistcoat with gilt buttons; his thin hair was brushed up over his temples, and his face was thin and pale. He received his visitor somewhat pompously, and made him a very slight bow. Mr. Simnel returned the salute much in the same fashion, and said, " You will wonder what has brought me to call on you, Mr. Townshend?"

" I—I am not aware what can have procured me the honour of a visit, Mr.—Mr.—" and the

old gentleman held up Mr. Simnel's card at arm's-
length, and looked at it through his double eye-
glass.

" Simnel's my name! I daresay it conveys to
you no meaning whatsoever?"

" Oh, I beg your pardon! On the contrary,
your name is familiar to me as that of the secretary of the Tin-Tax Office. I am glad to make
your acquaintance, sir. I often have communi-
cation with official men. What can I do for you?"

" It's in a private capacity that I've come to
see you," said Mr. Simnel. " I heard you were
going out of town, and I had something special
to talk over with you."

" I must trouble you to be concise and quick,"
said Mr. Townshend, by no means relishing the
easy manner of his visitor. " As you say, I am
going out of town,—for the benefit of my health,
—and every moment is precious."

" I shall not detain you very long," said Simnel, who had begun to nurse his leg, to Mr. Townshend's intense disgust. " I suppose we're private
here? You'll excuse me; but you'll be glad of it

before I've done. I may as well be brief in what I have to say; it will save both of us trouble. To begin with: I'm not by origin a London man. I come from Combcardingham; so do you."

Mr. Townshend's cheeks paled a little as he said, " I came from Calcutta, sir."

" Yes; last, I know; but you went to Calcutta, and from Combcardingham."

" I never was in the place in my life."

" Weren't you, indeed? then it must have been your twin-brother. I know a curious story about him, which I'll tell you."

" If you are come here to fool away my time, sir!"—said Mr. Townshend, rising.

" By no means, my dear sir. You don't know me personally; but I'll pledge my official reputation that the story is worth hearing. I think when I mention the names of Pigott and Wells—"

Down at last—sunk down cowering in his chair, just as at the Schröders' dinner, when he heard those dreadful names.

" Ah, I thought you would remember them. Well, Pigott and Wells were wool-merchants of old standing in Combcardingham. Pigott had long been dead; but Wells carried on the business of the firm under the old name. His solicitors were Messrs. Banner and Blair. One day Mr. Banner came to their articled clerk, and said to him, 'Robert, I have got an awkward business on hand; but you're a sharp fellow and can be trusted. Old Wells is coming here presently *with some one else.* I shall want a signature witnessed; but I'll get Podmore to do that. All you have to do is to keep your eyes against that window,' pointing to a pane hidden behind a curtain; 'and mark all you see, specially faces. It may be a lesson to you on a future occasion.'"

"Well, sir?" interrupted Townshend.

"Well, sir, the clerk placed himself as directed, and saw old Mr. Wells and a thick-set, dissipated-looking man shown into the room. Banner told Mr. Wells he was prepared for him, and produced a paper for signature; the signer of which, in consideration of Mr. Wells consenting to forego prosecuting him for the forgery of a bill of 120*l.* attached to the document, promised to leave

England and never to return. You're interested now; I thought you would be. Podmore was called in, and witnessed the dissipated young man sign the paper; but he knew nothing of its contents. Then old Wells, raising his shaking fore-finger, said, 'For your poor mother's sake, sir; not for yours!' and the dissipated-looking man drew a long breath, as though a great weight were off his mind, and strode out. The articled clerk saw all this, and marked the features of the forger; he did not see him again for many years. He sees him now!"

"What do you mean?"

"Simply, that you were the forger, I the clerk!"

"But that paper—that horrible confession, and the bill, they are destroyed! Wells swore he would destroy them before his death!"

"He intended to do so, but he died suddenly, poor old man; and in going through his desk I found them. I've got them here!"

"And what use are they to you? What harm are they to me? I shall swear—"

"Stop a minute! Podmore is alive; he's got
Banner and Blair's business in Combcardingham
now; he would verify his signature any day, and
yours too. No; I fairly tell you I've thought of
it all for several years, and I don't see your loop-
hole. I think I've got you tight!" And Mr.
Simnel smiled pleasantly as he squeezed his thumb
and forefinger together, as though he were chok-
ing a rabbit.

Mr. Townshend was cowering in his chair,
and had covered his face with his hands. When
he raised it, he was livid. "What do you want?
—money?"

"No," said Simnel, "not exactly. Oddly
enough, I want nothing at present! I merely
wanted, as you were going out of town, to set
matters straight, and let us understand each other
before you left. I'll let you know when I really
require you to do something for me, and you'll not
fail, eh?" These last words rather sharply.

"In all human—I mean—in a—" and the old
man stammered, broke down, and threw himself
back in his chair, sobbing violently.

"Come, come!" said Simnel; "don't take on so! You'll not find me hard; but you know in these days one must utilise one's opportunities. There, good-by! you won't forget my name; and I'll write here when I want you."

And he touched, not unkindly, the shrinking old man's shoulder, and went out.

CHAPTER XI.

WEAVING THE WEB.

In his well-deserved character of prudent campaigner, Mr. Simnel took no immediate steps to avail himself of the signal advantage which he had gained in his interview with Mr. Townshend. That eminent British merchant went abroad, and his name was recorded among a choice sprinkling of fashionables as honouring the steamship *Baron Osy*, bound for Antwerp, with their presence, and, on the "better-day-better-deed" principle, selecting the Sunday as the day of their departure. Mr. Simnel read the paragraph with a placid smile; he had seen sufficient of Mr. Townshend in that interview to guess that his illness was merely the result of care and worry, and that there was no reason to apprehend his proximate death. Antwerp—doubtless thence Brussels, the

Rhine, and perhaps Switzerland—would make a
pleasant tour; and as for any idea of escape, he
knew well enough that that thought had never
crossed Mr. Townshend's mind. The old gentleman knew he would have to pay the possessor
of his secret heavily in one way or another, but
in what he was as yet totally ignorant; besides,
his business engagements in London utterly prevented all chance of his retiring in any sudden
manner. And so Mr. Simnel remained quietly
at his post at the Tin-Tax Office, apparently not .
taking any notice of any thing save the regular
business routine, but in reality intent on his
earnest cat-like watching of all around him, and
always ready to pull any string at what he considered the proper opportunity.

He kept his eyes on Mr. Beresford, and knit
his eyebrows very much as he contemplated that
gentleman's proceedings. Whether prompted by
anxiety for the fate of his eight-hundred pounds
loan or by some other occult reason, Mr. Simnel
had been specially watchful over the Commissioner, and urged upon him to bring the specu-

lation in which he had embarked to a prosperous close. With this view he had dissuaded Beresford from going to Scotland, whither, as usual, he was bound on his autumnal excursion; representing to him that he had of late been very lax in his attendance; that he had had much more leave of absence than any of his brother commissioners; that Sir Hickory Maddox had once or twice referred to the subject in any thing but a complimentary manner; and that the best thing he could do to stave off an impending row would be to volunteer to stop in town, and let the other members of the board have a chance of running away in the fine weather. At this suggestion Mr. Beresford looked very black and waxed very wroth, and couldn't see why the deuce, and on his oath couldn't tell the necessity, &c.; but relented somewhat when his friend pointed out to him that there was no necessity for his attending more than twice a week at the office, just to sign such papers as were pressing; and that instead of remaining in his South-Audley-Street lodgings, he could go out and take rooms at a beautiful little inn in the village of Whittington, where there was a glorious cook, a capital cellar, beautiful air, splendid prospect, and above all, which was twenty minutes' canter from the Uplands, Schröder's summer place. To this plan Mr. Beresford consented; and after asking for a further loan of fifty, and getting five-and-twenty, from Simnel, Beresford and his mare Gulnare were domesticated at the Holly Bush, and he prepared to make play.

But somehow the state of affairs did not please Mr. Simnel. One day, when he and Mr. and Mrs. Schröder were Beresford's guests, he seemed specially annoyed; and on the next occasion of his friend's visiting the office, he took the opportunity of speaking to him.

"I want to say a word to you, Master Charles," said he, entering the board-room and addressing Beresford, who was stretched on the sofa reading the *Post*, and envying the sportsmen whose bags were recorded therein. "I want to know how you're getting on."

"Getting on! in what way?" asked Beresford, putting down the paper and lazily looking round; "as regards money, do you mean? because, if so, I could take that other five-and-twenty from you with a great amount of satisfaction."

"You're very good," said Simnel, with a sardonic grin: "but I'd rather not. I'm afraid you've been trying some of Dr. Franklin's experiments with kites again recently; at all events, I've seen several letters addressed to you in Parkinson's — of Thavies Inn, I mean — handwriting; which looks any thing but healthy. However, I didn't mean that; I meant in the other business—the great venture."

"Oh," said Beresford, "that's all right."

"I'm glad to hear it. Satisfactory, and all that sort of thing, eh?"

"Perfectly. Why do you ask?"

"Well, to tell you the truth," said Simnel, with that kind of honest bluntness, that inexpressible frankness, generally assumed by a man who is going to say something disagreeable, "I

had an idea that it was quite the opposite. When
we dined with you the other day,—deuced good
dinner it was too; I was right to recommend
you there, wasn't I? I haven't tasted such
spitchcocked eels for years; and that man's
moselle has a finer faint flavour of the muscat
than any I know in England,—when we dined
with you, as I say, I fancied things were all
wrong with the lady. I talked to the old boy, as
in duty bound, and listened to all his platitudes
about the influence of money—as though I didn't
know about that, good lord! But the whole time
I was listening, and chiming in here and there
with such interjections as I thought appropriate,
I kept my eye on you and madam; and from
what I saw, I judged it wasn't all plain sailing.
I was right; wasn't I?"

"Well," said Mr. Beresford, between his
teeth, "you were, and that's the truth. We've
come to grief somehow; but how, I can hardly
tell. It was going on splendidly; I had followed all your instructions to the letter, and,
in fact, I was thoroughly accepted as her brother,

when she suddenly veered round; and though I
can't say she's been unkind, yet she has lost all
that warmth that so pleasantly characterised her
regard; and now, I think, rather avoids me than
otherwise."

"You've not overdone it, have you? Not
been lapsing into your old style of flirtation,
and—"

"No; on my honour, no. I rather think
some of her friends have been putting the moral
screw on. You recollect a Miss Lexden—Mrs.
Churchill that is now?"

"Perfectly! But *she* would not be likely to
object to a flirtation."

"Not as mademoiselle, but as madame she
has rangéed herself, and I believe her husband's
a straight-laced party. She was up at Uplands
for a couple of days, and rather snubbed me
when I presented myself there in my fraternal
character. I've been putting things together
in my mind, and I begin to think that Mrs.
Schröder's coldness dated from Mrs. Churchill's
visit."

"Likely enough. I daresay Mrs. Churchill goes in tremendously now for all the domestic virtues. If a reformed rake makes the best husband, a penitent flirt ought to make the best wife; and, by all accounts, Miss Barbara Lexden was a queen of the art. I hear that she and her husband lead a perpetually billing-and-cooing existence, like a pair of genteelly-poor turtles, in some dovecot near Gray's Inn."

"That man Lyster's been a good deal to the house lately, too. I always hated that fellow, and I know he hates me; he looks at me sometimes as though he could eat me. Schröder seems to have taken a fancy to him; and I sometimes half fancy that he has a kind of spooney attachment to Mrs. Schröder—if you recollect, I told you I thought he was after her when we were all down at Bissett—though I don't think very much of that. I'll tell you what it is, Simnel," continued Mr. Beresford, in a burst of confidence, struggling up into a sitting position on the sofa, and beating his legs with the folded newspaper as he spoke, "I'm getting devilish sick of all this dodging and duffing, and I've been thinking seriously of calling my creditors together, getting them to take so much a-year, and then going in quietly and marrying Kate Mellon after all."

Mr. Simnel's face flushed but for an instant; it was its normal colour when he said,

"You're mad! You, with the ball at your foot, to think of such a course! So much a-year, indeed! Butchers and bakers do that sort of thing, I believe, when they've been let in; but not forty-per-cent men; not money-lending insurance-offices. Breathe a hint of your state, and they'd be down upon you at once, and sell you up like old sticks. Besides, you couldn't come to any arrangement with your creditors without its leaking out somehow. It would get into those infernal trade-circulars, or protection-gazettes, or whatever they're called; and if the Bishop or Lady Lowndes heard of it, all your chances of inheriting in either of those quarters would be blown to the winds. As to—to Kate Mellon, you may judge how your alliance with her would please either of the august persons I have named."

"Jove! you're right," said Beresford, biting his nails.

"Right, of course I am ; and here you've only to wait, and an heiress—a delightful little creature to boot—is absolutely thrown into your arms. You're a child, Charley, in some things,—you clever men always have a slate off somewhere, you know,—and in business you're a positive child. Can't you see that yours must be a waiting race?—that you mustn't mind being hustled, and bothered, and cramped, at the beginning, but must always keep your eyes open for your chance, and then make the running? The least impetuosity, such as you hint at, would throw away every hope, and destroy a very excellently planned scheme. Oh, you needn't wince at the word ; we are all schemers in love, as well as in every thing else, if we only acknowledged it."

"Then you counsel my keeping on still, and endeavouring to regain my influence?"

"Certainly ; by all means. It will come back,

never fear. And look here, Charley; don't fall
into that horribly common and vulgar error of
abusing the people who are supposed to be thwart-
ing your plans. Be specially kind, on the contrary, in all you say of them. This Captain Lyster,
for instance, I should proclaim, if I were you, a
thorough gentleman—a preux chevalier of a type
now seldom seen—a man evidently smothering
an unhappy passion for—for—any body but Mrs.
Schröder. Wouldn't the other one do? Mrs.
Churchill, I mean."

"Do! What do you mean? There used certainly to be a flirtation between them at one time,
and—"

"Quite enough. Only keep Mrs. Schröder from
the notion that Lyster is spooning her; for that's
enough at once to turn her silly little thoughts to
him. Speak kindly of every one; and don't show
the smallest signs of weariness, depression, or dis-
couragement."

When Mr. Simmel returned to his own room,
he settled himself down into his chair, and fell

to nursing his leg and thinking, with the old sinister smile on his face.

"He's not the easiest fellow in the world to deal with—Beresford! At least, he'd be difficult to some; but I think I've got him in hand. Wants every thing to run slick off the reel at once, the idiot! As though any great coup had ever been pulled off, save by waiting, and watching, and patience. Marry Kate Mellon, indeed!" and here Mr. Simnel's fingers, intertwined across his knee, cracked as he pulled at them—"marry Kate Mellon, and with such a damned air of patronage too! No, my young friend, never! You held a trump-card there, and you neglected to play it; and in my game there's no revoking. I must see Kitty, and look how the land lies. I think I've stalled Master Charley off for some little time; and it's no good bringing about an éclaircissement of the Schröder business; which Kitty would be safe to do so soon as she had any tangible proofs. Then I should lose my eight hundred pounds in Charley Beresford's general and helpless smash. But I'd sooner drop them than miss my chance of

Kitty. Slippery, though—slippery as the deuce!" and Mr. Simnel put his elbow on his knee, and his face into his hand, and sat plucking at his chin: "hankers after Beresford, no doubt,—I think has a liking for that young Prescott; but that I'll put a stop to to-day,—and I suppose only thanks me for my kindness. And yet I can put the finishing stroke to the whole thing in one moment; only want the one connecting-link and the story's complete; and then I'll take my oath she'll have me. I'll ride up there this afternoon, and just see how the land lies."

In accordance with this determination, Mr. Simnel that afternoon mounted his thoroughbred and cantered off to The Den. He found the mistress of the house at home, seated on a rustic seat, in a little grass-plot in front of the drawing-room window, with a carriage-whip in her hand, with which she was flicking the heads off such flowers as were within reach. She had evidently just come in from a drive, for she still wore her bonnet and black-lace shawl, though the former was perched on the top of her head, to keep off the sun, while the latter hung trailing down her back. She had altered in appearance, and not for the better: her eyes were unnaturally bright; her cheeks sunken, and marked here and there with hectic patches. Simnel gave his horse to a groom, and walked up the garden-path. Kate Mellon looked up at the sound of his advancing footsteps; at first vacantly enough, but when she recognised him, she roused herself, and got up to meet him.

"How are you, Simnel?" she said, with outstretched hand. "I was thinking of you only to-day, and wondering what had become of you. It's ages since you've been up here."

"I've been very busy, Kate, and been unable to come. You know my wish is to come as frequently as possible; oh, you needn't shake your head, because you are quite certain of it; but that's neither here nor there. I keep to my portion of the contract, and shall not bore you about myself until I've shown you I've a right to ask you to listen to me. And now, how are you, and what are you doing? To tell truth, I don't think you look very bonny, young woman: a little dragged, eh? End of the season, perhaps?"

"Oh, I'm all right!" said Kate, hurriedly; "never better in health, and jolly; that's the great point, isn't it, Simnel, eh? I'm learning to look after number one, you know; and when you can do that, you're all right, ain't you? Have some lunch? No? then look here; I've got something you must taste,—some wonderful Madeira. Oh, all right; I know it'll put some colour into your cheeks, and do you good."

She called to a passing servant, and the wine was brought,—rare old tawny, full-bodied, mellow Madeira,—such wine as is now to be met in about a dozen houses in the land, and utterly different from the mixture of mahogany-shavings and brandy which is sold under its name. Simnel poured out two half-glasses; but Kate took the decanter from him, filled her glass to the brim, and nodding to him, drank off half its contents.

"Ah!" said she, with a long-drawn inspiration; "that's the stuff! No nonsense in that, you know: doesn't pretend to be what it isn't, and can't deceive you. Tom Gillespie sent me a lot of that: found no end of it in the cellars of his old uncle, the East-India Director, whose tin he came in for. I find it does me good, steadies my nerve, and gives me fresh life. What are you shaking your head at?"

"It's dangerous tipple, Kate. I don't like to hear you talk like that. Your nerves used to be as strong as steel, without any steadying. I say, Kitty," said Mr. Simnel with a grave face; "you're not giving way to this sort of thing for—"

"For what?" interrupted Kate, with a discordant laugh; "for comfort? Oh, no, thank you; I don't want that yet: I don't want to drown my sorrows in the bowl. I haven't got any sorrows, and I shouldn't do that with them if I had. By the way, Simnel, how is that affair going on,—you know what I mean? You promised to let me know."

"I believe it stands very much the same as it did," said he.

"Then it hasn't worn out yet? he isn't tired of it, eh?" she asked eagerly.

"No; it still goes on."

"You promised to tell me the woman's name, Simnel; why haven't you done so? You pretend friendship for me, and then you keep things from me that I ought to know; and you don't come and see me, and—There, I don't believe in you a bit!"

"I keep things from you until the proper time for you to know them. I don't come and see you, because all the leisure time I have had has been devoted to your interests; and, by the way, Kate, that brings me to the occasion of my present visit. I suppose you give me credit for sincerity—"

"Oh, ah; well, what then?"

"I mean that you believe in me sufficiently to think that any step I should take, any question I should ask, would not be out of mere idle curiosity; but because I thought they would be beneficial to you?"

She nodded her head, and stretched her hand towards the decanter; but seeing Simnel frown, she stopped short, took up the whip which lay close by, and commenced flicking the flowers again.

"I want to ask you about your people,"—the girl started;—"who they are; where you came from; what you know of them."

"You know all that fast enough,—from York-shire,—you've heard me say before. What more's wanted to be known? I pay my way, don't I, and who does more? I'm not required to show my christening certificate to every one that wants a horse broke, I suppose?"

"What a fiery child it is!" said Simnel. "No one has a right to ask any thing at all about it, —I least of all; but I think,—and I am not sanguine, you know,—that I shall be able, if you will confide in me, to help you very greatly in the most earnest wish of your life."

"Stop!" exclaimed Kate; "do you know what that is?"

"I think I do," said Simnel, looking at her kindling eyes, quivering nostril, and twitching lips.

"If not, I'll tell you; I don't mind telling you: revenge on Charles Beresford! revenge! revenge!" and at each repetition of the word, she slashed savagely at the tall flowers near her.

"Well, I think I might say I could help you in that," said Simnel quietly; "but you must be frank. You know I'm a man of the world; and I've made it my business to go a little into this question. So now tell me your life, from the first that you can remember of it."

"You're a cool hand, Simnel; but I know you mean running straight, so I don't mind. First thing of all I can recollect is being held out at arm's length by Phil Fox, as the child in his great trick-act of Rolla, or the something of Peru. The circus belonged to old Fox, Phil's father; and I used to live with the Foxes,—the old man and woman and Bella Fox, and Phil and his wife. Bad lot she was: had been a splendid rider, but fell and broke her leg; and was always vicious and snappish, and that irritating, I wonder Phil could put up with her. They were very kind to me, the Foxes, and I was quite like their own child; and I played fairies, and flower-girls, and columbines, and such like, all on horseback, in all the towns we went circuit. I used to ask the old man sometimes about myself; but he never would say more than that I was his little apprentice, and I should find it all right some day. And so I went on with them till I grew quite a big girl, and used to do the barebacked-steed business, and what I liked better, the riding-habit and the highly-trained charger dodge, until old Fox declared there was no better rider in England than me. I was just nineteen, when he sent for me one night,—it was at Warwick, I recollect, and we'd had a stunning house,—and I found him with two gentlemen standing with him. He pointed to one of them, and he said to me: 'Express'—that's the name he used to call me,— 'Express, this is the gentleman that bound you 'prentice to me ever so many years ago. He's come to take you away now, and make your fortune.' I cried, and said I didn't want my fortune made, and that I wouldn't go; but after a long talk full of business, I saw it would be for my good, and I agreed. So this place was bought for me in my name, and here I've been ever since."

"And who were those gentlemen?"

"That's exactly what I can't tell you."

"Can't tell?"

"Won't, if you like it better. There, don't look vexed. I'll tell you this much, one of them was my uncle,—my real uncle, I firmly believe,—though on which side you must find out."

"And the other?"

"The other I love dearer than any one on earth."

"Dearer than you loved—"

"I know who you're going to say; infinitely dearer! but in—there; there's enough of that. One thing more I'll tell you: up to this hour I've never been told my father's name or rank in life."

"And this benevolent uncle did it all? Quite like a play, by Jove! Well, I've not learned much; but I may be able to make something of it—something that will be good for us both."

"That's all right! and now your business is finished?"

"Yes, entirely—no, not quite, by the way; I wanted to say one word to you on another subject. You know I'm not likely to be jealous, Kitty—"

"So far as I'm concerned, you've no right to be."

"I know, of course; but still one doesn't like these things. There's a young man named Prescott, who is in my office. I notice that he's constantly in your company; I've met you with him half-a-dozen times, and I hear frequently from others of his being with you."

"What of that?" she asked, with flushing cheek; "are you to settle my company for me?"

"Not at all—not at all; but I'm speaking both for your good and his. He's a young fellow of good abilities; but he's thoughtless and foolish, and, what's worse than all, he's poor. Now this riding about, horse-hiring and that sort of thing, necessarily leads him into expense; and from what I hear, he's going a great deal too fast. I hear all sorts of things about the young fellows who are under me, and I'm told that your friend Mr. Prescott is getting involved in money-matters; in fact, that he's mixed up in bill-transactions to an amount which, for him, is heavy, with a blood-sucking rascal named Scadgers, who is one of the pests of society in general, and government offices in particular."

"Scadgers!" replied Kate; "what a funny name! Scadgers, eh?"

"A good many people have found it any thing but a funny name, Kitty. Now, though I don't suppose there's any thing between you and Mr. Prescott—"

"Don't you trouble any more about that; perhaps you've never noticed that Mr. Prescott never is with me except when one of my pupils is there too: now do you understand?"

"There was no pupil nor any one else with you when I saw him talking to you in the Row some twelve months since; and he scuttled off as I rode up: however, I thought I'd warn you about him. He's on the downward road, and unless he pulls up, he'll come to grief; and it wouldn't do for you to be mixed up in any thing of that sort."

He sat some time longer talking of ordinary matters, and rattling on in his best style. In every thing he said there was a tinge of attention almost bordering on respect to his companion, which she did not fail to notice, and which decidedly impressed her in his favour. Indeed, Kate Mellon never had imagined that Mr. Simnel could have made such progress in her good graces as he did this day. They never recurred to any serious topic until his horse was brought, when just as he was mounting she touched him on the shoulder, and said, "You'll not forget to keep me up to the mark about that business?" then, with a half-shuddering laugh, "I'm still interested, you know, in that young man's progress." Simnel wheeled round and looked at her steadily under his bent eyebrows. "You shall be made acquainted with any thing that happens, depend upon it. Adieu!" and he sprang to the saddle, raised his hat, and rode slowly off.

" Not half cured yet," said he to himself, " not
half; and yet so savage at his slight, that she'd do
him any bad turn on the spur of the moment, and
repent of it instantly. She was telling truth about
Prescott, I know; but it was best to break up that
instantly. How lovely she looked! a little flushed,
a little excited; but that only added to her charm.
I didn't like that Madeira being so handy, by the
way; I must look after that. By Jove, what a
fairy it is! where's there one to compare to her?
so round and plump and well put together! And
if I can only square this family history—uncle, eh?
who the deuce can that have been? That's an important link in the chain. And somebody she loves,
too; what the deuce does that mean? Ah, well,
it's coming to a head now: another month ought
to enable me to pull up the curtain on the last act
of the drama."

And Kate returned to her garden-chair as the
sound of the horse's hoofs died away in the distance; and throwing herself back, and drumming
with her fingers upon the little table, went off into

a reverie. She thought of her devotion to Beresford; how the passion had first grown when he
first knew her; how she had given way to it; and
how the nourishment of it was one of the brightest
phases in her strange odd life. She remembered
the first time she saw him, the first compliment he
paid her; the way in which his easy jolly behaviour
struck her as compared with the dreary vapidity,
or, what was worse, the slangy fastness of the
other men of her acquaintance. And then she
thought of that eventful evening when she had
knelt at his feet and—she dashed her clenched
fist upon the table as she remembered that, and
shuddered and bit her lips when she thought
that a description of that scene had been given
amid ribald shouts. Mr. Simnel had not so much
share of her thoughts as probably he would have
wished; but she pondered for a few moments on
his eagerness to obtain particulars of her early
life, and wondered what scheme he had in hand.
She had a very high opinion of his intellect, and
felt sure he was using it just then in her service;
but she could not conceive to what end his labours

were tending. And then she remembered what he had said about Mr. Prescott; and her face grew a little sad.

"Poor Jim!" she said to herself; "poor fellow! going to grief is he? in debt and dropping his money, like a young fool as he is. And that nice girl, too, so fresh and jolly and countrified and innocent! Lord help us! What are you at, Kitty, you idiot! why should those things give you a twinge? Steady now; it's not often your heart buck-jumps like that. They'll go all right, those though, if Jim can only be put square. And that he shall be! What's the use of my hoarding in my old stocking; it'll never be any good to me; and so I may as well have the pleasure of helping somebody else. Scadgers, that was the name; I'll get that put right at once. Scadgers! I wonder where he lives. However, that'll be easily found out. Poor Jim! what a good husband he'll make that rosy-faced girl."

What was it that made Kate Mellon's head drop on her hands, and the tears ooze through the fingers covering her eyes? Not the thought of

Mr. Prescott's marrying some one else surely, for had she not resolutely snubbed his proposals? Certain it is that she remained with her head bowed for full ten minutes, and that when she looked up, her face was tear-dabbled and her eyes red and swollen. She took no heed of her appearance, however, but walked into the house, and pulling out her gaudy blotting-book, she scrawled a long letter, which, when finished, she addressed to " F. Churchill, Esq., *Statesman* Office, E.C."

CHAPTER XII.

TIGHTENING THE CURB.

THE garden-party at Uplands had a serious effect
on the household in Great Adullam Street. Of
course the actual disturbance, the state of warfare
engendered by what Frank Churchill imagined he
had seen take place between his wife and Captain
Lyster in the shrubbery, did not last long. When
Barbara swept up to her bedroom from the hired
brougham, Frank retreated into his little snuggery
and lit his old meerschaum-pipe, and sat gazing vacantly through the smoke-wreaths, and pondering
on the occurrences of the day. He could scarcely
realise to himself what had passed; he could scarcely
imagine that the woman to whom, twelve months
since, he had sworn fealty, whose lightest whisper
caused his pulse to throb, and who, on her part,
had changed the whole style and current of her life

for the sake of fulfilling her determination to be his
and his alone, could have so far repented of that
great crisis in her career as to listen to the compliments of another man, to receive, with evident
satisfaction, his unqualified admiration, and to fly
off in a rage, with fire in her eyes and bitter words
on her lips, when her husband remonstrated with
her on her conduct. Here were they, that " twain
one flesh," that mysterious two-in-one, sitting
under the same roof indeed, but in separate
rooms; each thinking hard thoughts of the other,
each with anger rife against the other, and with
harsh words applied to each other yet ringing in
their ears. Great Heavens! thought Frank, was
this what he had fondly pictured to himself? Was
this the quiet haven of repose, the lodge in the vast
wilderness of Mesopotamia, with one fair spirit for
his minister, on which he had so rashly reckoned?
Was the lodge to be a divided territory? and was
the fair spirit to be equally fair to some other man,
and to be a minister of the blatant, reviling, Boa-
nerges class? Instead of the quiet and rest on
which he had calculated, and which were so neces-

sary to him after his exciting hard work, was his mind to be racked by petty jealousies, his peace invaded by wretched squabbles, the sunshine of his existence overclouded with gloom and doubt? Was his wife to be an adversary instead of a helpmate? were her— And then abruptly he stopped in his self-torturing, as he thought of her,—how friendless and unprotected she was, how he alone was her prop and stay in the world ; and then he turned the whole matter in his mind, and it occurred to him that that horribly irritable temper of his might have led him again into mischief, causing him to see things that really might not have happened, and to use language far stronger than there was any necessity for, and to render him violent and undignified and absurd, and so completely to do away with the force accruing from his right position. For undoubtedly he was in the right position; for had he not seen with his own eyes— what? They were walking together, certainly ; but there was no reason why that should not be : fifty other couples were promenading the same grounds at the same time, and—no! on reflection, he did

not see Lyster kiss her hand; it was that young
idiot who was gabbling to him the whole time, and
who said something about it. Perhaps nothing
of the kind had occurred. Barbara had denied
it instantly; and when had she ever breathed
a falsehood to him? She was not the style of
woman to equivocate; her pride would save her
from that; and—it must have been all fancy! some
horrible mistake, out of which had arisen this
wretched scene and his worse than wretched rage.
And now there was something between them, some
horrible misunderstanding which must be at once
set right. If—if any thing were to happen to
either of them, and one were to die while there was
enmity, or something like it, existing between them!
and this thought caused the meerschaum to be laid
aside unfinished, and sent Frank striding up, four
stairs at a time, to his bedroom.

He found Barbara sitting in her white dressing-
gown, arranging her hair before the looking-glass.
Her face was very white, her eyelids a little red
and puffed, and her lips were tightly pressed together. She took no notice of the opening of the

door, but went calmly on with her toilet. Frank was a little disconcerted by this; he had calculated on a tender look of recognition, a few smothered words of explanation, and a final tableau in each other's arms. But as Barbara, with the greatest serenity, still appeared completely immersed in the intricate plaiting evolutions she was performing with a piece of her hair and a stalwart hair-pin, Frank advanced gently, and standing behind her chair, touched her shoulder and said softly, " Darling !"

There was no reply; but the hands occupied in the plaiting manœuvre perhaps shook a little.

" My darling," repeated Frank, " won't you notice me ?"

" Were you speaking to me ?" asked Barbara in an icy voice, and looking up at him with a calm rigid blank face.

" To whom else should I be speaking ? to whom else should I apply that term ?"

" Really I can't say. The last time you spoke to me, you were good enough to swear; and as I know you pride yourself on your consistency, I could not imagine you could so soon alter your tone."

"No; but, Barbara dearest, you should not throw that in my teeth; you know that I was vexed; that I—"

"Vexed, Frank! Vexed! I wonder at you! You accuse me of something utterly untrue, in language such as I have never listened to before; and then, as an excuse, you plead that you were vexed!"

"I was foolish, Barbara, headstrong and horrible, and let my confounded temper get the mastery over me; but then, child, you ought to forgive me; for all I did was from excess of love for you. If I did not hang upon every word, every action, of yours, I should be far less exacting in my affection. You should think of that, Barbara."

His voice was broken as he spoke, and she noticed that the hand which was upon her chairback shook palpably.

"You *could* not have meant what you said in the brougham, Frank," said she in a softened tone. "You could not have imagined that I should have permitted—there, I cannot speak of it!" she exclaimed abruptly, placing her handkerchief to her swimming eyes.

"No, my darling, I will not. I could not—I never—of course—fool that I am!" and then incoherently, but satisfactorily, the question was dismissed.

Dismissed temporarily, but by no means forgotten, by no means laid aside by either of them. Captain Lyster called the next day while Frank was at the office, eager to see whether Mrs. Churchill had repented of the task she had undertaken in counselling and warning Alice Schröder; and Barbara told her husband on his return of the visit she had had, and mentioned it with eyes which a desire not to look conscious rendered somewhat defiant, and with cheeks which flushed simply because it was the last thing they ought to have done. Heaven knows Barbara Churchill had nothing to be ashamed of in being visited by Captain Lyster. She never had the smallest sign of a feeling stronger than friendship for him, and yet she felt somewhat guilty, as she acknowledged to herself that his visit had given her very great pleasure. The truth was that the garden-party at Uplands had completely upset the current of Barbara's life. When, in the first wild passion of her love for him who became her husband, she had willingly forfeited all that had hitherto been the pleasure of her life,—the luxury and admiration in which she had been reared, the pleasant surroundings which had been hers since her cradle,—she had found something in exchange. She had given up half-a-hundred friendships, which she knew to be hollow and empty; but she had consoled herself with one vast love, which she believed to be lasting and true, and which, after all, was a novelty.

As has been said, Barbara had had her flirtations innumerable, but she had never known before what love was; and having a very sensitive organisation, and going in heart and soul for the new passion, she had not in any great degree, at all events, felt the alteration in her position. Although every thing was different and

inferior, every thing was in some degree connected with him, who was paramount in her idea
to any thing she had ever known. She might
feel the dulness of the neighbourhood, the small-
ness of the house, the difference in the society
and in her own occupations and amusements;
but all these were part and parcel of that sun
of her existence—her husband; that great lumi-
nary, in whose brilliant rays all little gloom-
spots were swallowed up and merged. Even
when the glamour died away, and the black-
nesses stood out in bold relief, she had been so
dazed by the brightness, and, owing to the thorough change, the events of her past life seemed
so far away, as to awaken but very little remorse
or regret. She was beginning to bear with something like patience the prosiness of her mother-in-
law, the spiteful criticisms of Mrs. Harding, the
hideous vulgarity of some of her other neighbours. But the visit to Uplands came upon her
as a terrific shock. Once more mixing in her
old society, hearing the fashionable jargon to
which she had been accustomed from her youth

up; meeting those who had always looked up to
her as their superior in beauty, and consequently
in marketable value; listening to soft compliments; seeing her wishes, ever so slightly hinted,
obeyed with alacrity; breathing once more that
atmosphere in which she was reared, but from
which she seemed to have been long estranged,—
Barbara felt more and more like Barbara Lexden,
while Barbara Churchill faded hazily away. The
dull, dull street,—the dead, dead life,—the poverty which prescribed constant care in the household management,—the dowdy dresses and second-
hand manners of the inhabitants of the quarter,—
the daily vexations and cares and wrong-way rub-
bings,—seemed all to belong to some hideous
dream, while the real existence passed into the former life with a pleasant addition in the person of
Frank. The pleasure was brief enough, and she
woke to all the horrors rendered doubly bitter by
the short renewal of bygone joys. The clock had
struck twelve, the ballroom had vanished, and she
was again Cinderella with haunting memory for
her glass-slipper. The prince remained, certainly;

but he was no longer a prince; he had bad tempers, and was peevish and jealous, and thoroughly mortal. She had returned to the dust and dreariness of Great Adullam Street, and the rattling cabs, and Mrs. Churchill in her old black-silk dress, and the Hebrews opposite smoking their cigars at the open windows in the hot summer evenings. She could scarcely fancy that there was a world where people dressed in full muslin, and pink-crape bonnets, or bewitching hats; where business was unknown, and work never heard of; where there were perpetual croquet-parties and picnics and horticultural fêtes; where there were night-drives homeward in open carriages after Richmond dinners; and where the men talked of something else than when Brown was going to bring out his poems, or what a slating Smith's novel had had in the *Scourge*. In that brief respite from her weary life, she had heard those around her talking of their plans to be carried out on the then occurring break-up of the season; she had heard girls talk with rapture of their approaching visits to German Spas and Italian lakes; she had heard arrangements made for meeting in English country-houses, where she had formerly been an eagerly sought-for guest; or at fashionable seabords, where she had been the reigning belle. And she came back with the full knowledge that a fortnight's run to some cockney watering-place, handy of access to London, where she could live in cheap lodgings and play a very undistinguished part, would be all the relaxation she could possibly hope for. And all this sunk into her soul, and made her wretched and discontented, and formed the wandering isles of night which dashed the very source and fount of her day.

It was wrong, undoubtedly. She had chosen her course, and must run it; as the Mesopotamians would have expressed themselves, she had made her bed, and must lie upon it. She had her husband to think of, and should have struggled womanfully to bear up against all these small crosses and disquietudes for his sake; she should have met her fate with a brave heart, and striven to prevent his having any suspicion of the longings and disappointments by which she was racked. Barbara should have done all this, as we in our different way should have done so much, which we have resolutely omitted,—paid that bill, for instance; avoided that woman; not bought that horse; helped that old friend; denied ourselves that fling in print at Jones. She should have done; but, like us, she didn't. Her character was any thing but perfect; and the very pride on which she so much prided herself, and which should have left her straight, now turned against herself, and, "like a hedgehog rolled the wrong way," pricked her mercilessly. She did indeed struggle to contend with the feelings which were conquering her, and which were the "little low" sensations renewed with tenfold force; but without success. A dead dull despair, a loathing and detestation of all the circumstances of her life, a horror of the people round her, and a wild regret for what had gone before never to return,—these were the demons which beset Barbara's daily path. And with them at one time came the first threatenings of another feeling which would have been more destructive to all chance of present or future happiness than any other, had not Providence in its mercy counteracted its effect by a passion, bad indeed, torturing, and hurtful, but nothing like so deadly as the other. Weighed down by her real or fancied misery, constantly repining in secret, and comparing her present with her past life, Barbara might have been tempted to think of Frank as the agent of her wretchedness, as the primary mover in the chain of events which had made her exchange Tyburnia for Great Adullam Street, luxury for comparative poverty, and happiness for despair; she might have done this, but she became jealous. She noticed that lately Frank's manner had been strange and preoccupied; that he was away from home very much more frequently than when they were first married; that from what she gathered when she heard him talking with his friends, he evidently sought work which took him out, and on two or three occasions had gone on country trips in the interest of the journal—duty which did not fall to his lot, and which he had never undertaken before. His manner to her, she thought, was certainly very much changed, and she did not like the alteration. He was courteous always, and gentle; but he had gradually lost all that petting fondness which, from its very rarity in a man of his stamp, was so winning at first; and with his courtesy was mingled a grave sad air, which Barbara understood to mean reproach, and which galled her mightily. I do not know that Barbara at first really felt jealous of her husband: had she examined the foundation of her jealousy and sifted its causes, there is very little doubt that the natural sense which she undoubtedly possessed would have shown her that her suspicions were absurd. But the truth is, she all unwittingly rather encouraged the passion, as a relief from the monotonous misery of her life, without a thought of how rapidly it grew, or what proportions it might eventually assume. It was a change to think differently of Frank, to take a feverish interest in his proceedings and in the proceedings of those with whom he was brought into contact; and Frank himself was surprised to find how the "little low" fits had been succeeded by a more sprightly demeanour—a demeanour which showed itself in sharp glances and bitter words.

And Frank, was he happy? In truth, not one whit happier than his wife, though his wretchedness sprang from a different cause and was shown in a different way. He felt that he had clutched the great prize, and found it to be a Dead-Sea apple; that he had reached the turning-point of his career, passed it, and found the rest of his course all down-hill; he had played the great stake of his life and lost it; and henceforward his heart's purse was empty, and he was bankrupt in affections. It had come upon him, gradually indeed, but with overwhelming force: at first he had ascribed Barbara's pettishness to the mere vagaries of a girl, and had looked upon her caprices as relics of that empire which had been hers so long, and from which she, naturally enough, was unwilling to part. He had seen, not without annoyance, indeed, but still without any deep or lasting pang, that there was an uncomfortable feeling, based either upon rivalry or some other passion equally unintelligible to him, between his wife and his mother; but he had hoped this would pass away. He had noticed that his old friends, though they spoke with warm admiration of Barbara's beauty, seemed to shirk any question of liking or being pleased with her; and that, let them meet her however often, she scarcely seemed to make any progress in their regard; but he thought this was as much their fault as hers, and that the estrangement would wear off. It was not until his mother had dropped her hint as to the frequency of Captain Lyster's visits, that Frank's mind began to be seriously disturbed; it was not until the scene at Uplands, of which he had been an unwilling spectator, and the subsequent scene with Barbara in the brougham, that he began to feel that his marriage had been a horrible mistake. Then all Barbara's "low" fits, all her silence, all the tears which he could see constantly welling up into her eyes, and kept back only by a struggle as palpable as the tears themselves; then the complaints of dulness and monotony—all poor Barbara's short-

comings, indeed, and they were not a few—were
ascribed to one source. She had known this man
in former days; he was of her society and set,
and had probably made love to her, as had
hundreds before; and Frank ground his teeth as
he thought how Barbara's reputation as a flirt,
and her attractive qualities as a coquette, had
been kindly mentioned to him by more than one
of her old friends. Some quarrel had probably
occurred between them; during which he Frank
had crossed her path, had fallen at her feet,—
dazed idiot that he was!—and she had raised him
up, and out of pique, had married him. That
was the story, Frank could swear to it! he turned
it over and over in his mind until he believed it
implicitly, and conjured up the different scenes
and passages, which made his blood boil and sent
him, with set teeth and scowling brow, stamping
through the long-echoing Mesopotamian squares,
to the intense wonder of the policeman and the
few passers-by in those dreary thoroughfares.
Only when he was quite alone, however, did he
in the least give way to his emotions. When he

was at home—where he and Barbara would now sit for hours without exchanging a word, and where the occasional presence of a third person rendered matters more horrible, compelling them to put on a ghastly semblance of affectionate familiarity—when he was at home, or down at the *Statesman* Office, where he could be thoroughly natural, he was moody, stern, and silent. His manner had lost that round jollity which had always characterised it, and his appearance was beginning to change: he was thinner; there were silver lines in the brown hair, and two or three deep lines round the eyes.

Of course his friends noticed all this, as friends notice every thing. Madly and blindly people go through life, imagining that their thoughts and actions are—some of them, at least—known but to themselves alone; whereas all of them—all such, at least, as they would prefer keeping secret—are public property, and as thoroughly patent as if they had been proclaimed from the market-place cross. You may go on in London living for years next door to a neighbour whose name you are unacquainted with, and whom you have never seen; but make him an acquaintance, give him some interest in you, and without your in the least suspecting it, he will find out the whole story of your life, will know all about the young lady with the fair hair in Wiltshire, the hundred pounds borrowed from Robinson, the disappointment at Uncle Prendergast's will—all the little things, in fact, which you thought were buried in your own bosom; and will sit down opposite you at table with an innocent ingenuous face, as though your affairs were the very last things with which he would trouble himself. We all do this, day by day, with the noblest hypocrisy, and receive from our dear intimate statements of facts which we know to be false, and warpings of statements which we know to be perverted, with " Indeeds !" and " Reallys ?" and head-noddings of outward acquiescence and mocking incredulity in our hearts. Barbara Churchill had been the one grand subject of conversation for the Mesopotamian gossips ever since her marriage: they had lived upon her, and found that she improved in flavour. Her appearance, her dress, her manners; what they were pleased to term her " stand-offishness ;" her short-comings as a housekeeper; her ignorance in the matter of mending under-linen ; her novel-reading and piano-playing—all these had been toothsome morsels, far more enjoyable than the heavy pies, the thick chops, and the sardines which figured in that horrible Mesopotamian meal known as a " thick tea ;" and had been picked to the very bone. And then, when it began to be whispered about— as it very soon did—that there were dissensions in the Churchill camp, that all did not go as smoothly as it should, and that, in fact, quarrels were rife—then came the crowning delight of the banquet, and the female portion of the Great-Adullam-Street community was nearly delirious with excitement. Although old Mrs. Churchill, from her kind-heartedness and simplicity, had always been a great favourite with her neighbours, she had no idea of the extent of her popularity until this period. Her little rooms were literally beset with female friends ; and she had invitations to tea-parties three-deep. To these invitations—

to as many of them, at least, as was possible—she invariably responded. By nature the old lady hated the character of a gossip, and would have been highly indignant had she been charged with any propensity for chattering; but easily impressible by those with whom she was brought into contact, she had acquired a little of the prevalent failing of the region, and moreover, she thought it her duty to tell all she knew about the then favourite subject, in order, as she phrased it, " that poor Frank's position might be set right." But if poor Frank's position was properly looked after, it must be acknowledged that poor Barbara received her meed of popular disapprobation. Not that her mother-in-law ever said one direct word of condemnation; old Mrs. Churchill was far too good a Christian willingly to start or give currency to harsh criticism, more especially on one so closely allied to her. But it was very difficult to absolve her son from blame without shifting the onus of the avowed quarrel on to the shoulders of her daughter-in-law; and when the ladies surrounding the tea-table, groaning over " poor Mr.

Churchill's" domestic woes, shook their cap-strings in virtuous indignation at her who had caused them, the old lady made but a feeble protest, which speedily closed in a string of doleful ejaculations. In the minds of the members of this Mesopotamian Vehmgericht, of which Mrs. Harding might be considered president, Barbara stood fully convicted of the charge which they had themselves brought against her. Her indolence, her carelessness, her " fal-lal ways," her pride and squeamishness had brought—only rather sooner than was expected — their natural result; and " isn't it better, my dear, to have a little less good looks and a little less fondness for jingling the piano and reading trashy novels, and keep a tidy house over your head and live happily with your husband ?"

The stories of all that passed in Churchill's house, collected with care from old Mrs. Churchill and her servant Lucy,—whose habitual puritanical taciturnity was melted by the course of events, and who gave way to that hatred against Barbara which she had felt from the first moment of seeing her,

—and duly dressed, illustrated, and annotated by Mrs. Harding, who had a special talent in that way, of course before long reached Mr. Harding's ears.

It is difficult to explain how that good fellow was affected by the news. He had the warmest personal regard for Frank, loving him with something of paternal fondness; he had always impressed him with the propriety of marriage, and had looked forward with real anxiety to the time when he should see his friend settled for life. Not until then, he thought, would those talents which he knew Frank possessed enable him to take his proper position in the world: what he did now was well enough; but it was merely the evanescent sparkle of his genius. Soberly settled down with a woman worthy of him, the real products of his intellect and his reading would come forth, and he would step into the first rank of the men of his time. And now it had all come to this! Frank was married; but he had made a wrong selection, and was a moody, discontented, blighted man. The aspect of affairs was horrible; and when told of their real condition by his wife, George Harding determined that he would exercise his prerogative of friend, and speak to Churchill on the subject.

Accordingly the next day when he saw Frank at the usual consultation at the office, Harding waited until the other man had left the room, and then, placing his hand affectionately on his friend's shoulder, said: " I want two minutes with you, Frank."

" Two hours, if you like, Harding; it's all the same to me," replied Churchill wearily.

" I want you to tell me what ails you,—what has worked such a complete change in you, physically and morally; or rather, I don't want you to tell me, for I know."

Churchill looked up defiantly with flushed cheeks, as he exclaimed, "What do you know? are my private affairs topics for the tittle-tattle of —there, God help me! I'm weak as water. Now I want to quarrel with my best friend!"

" No, you don't, old man; and you would get no quarrel out of me, if you wished it ever so much. But I can't bear this any longer; I can't bear to see you losing your health and your spirits; and wearing yourself out day by day as you are, without coming to the rescue. Let us look the matter boldly in the face at once. You're—you're not quite happy at home, Frank, eh?"

"Happy!" he echoed with a strange hollow laugh; "no, not entirely perhaps."

"Well, that's a bad thing; but it's curable. At all events, giving way to moping and misery won't help it. Many men have begun their married life in wretchedness, and emerged, when they least expected it, into sunshine. Here are two young people who have not known each other above a couple of months, both of whom have very possibly been spoiled beforehand, and they arrive each with their own particular stock of whims and fancies, which they declare shall be carried out by the other. It takes time to rub down all the angles and points, and to provide for the regular working of the machinery; and it is never done by a jump. You've fine material to work upon too; if Mrs. Churchill were vulgar or uneducated, or did not care for you, you would have great difficulties to contend with. But as she is exactly the reverse of all this, she ought to be easily managed. Don't you understand that in these matters one or the other must have the upperhand? and that one should be the husband! The supremacy once asserted, all works well; not until then, and generally the struggle, though sharp, is very short. Every thing is wrong, and the whole machine is out of gear. You've let her have her own way too much, my friend. You must tighten the curb and see the result."

"If you were a horseman, Harding," said Frank with a dreary smile, "you would know that tightening the curb sometimes produces the worst of rebellious vices—rearing!"

"Oh, no fear of that; no fear of that. Try it! You really must do something, Frank; I can't bear to see you giving way like this. You must assert yourself, my good fellow, and at once; for though it may be bad now, it will be ten times worse hereafter, and you'll bitterly rue not having taken my advice."

And George Harding went home and told his wife what he had done, and assured her that she would find matters speedily set to rights in Great Adullam Street now.

And Frank Churchill walked home, pondering on the advice he had just received and finally determining within himself to adopt it. He supposed he had been weak and wanting in proper self-respect. Harding was always the reflex of his wife's sentiments, and doubtless that whole set of wretched tabbies had been pitying him as a poor spiritless creature. He would take Harding's advice and bring the matter to an issue at once.

He went into his little study and had just seated himself at his desk to commence his work when Barbara entered the room. She was dressed in her bonnet and shawl; her eyes were swollen, and there were traces of recent tears still on her cheeks; the muscles round her mouth were working visibly, and her whole frame was quivering with excitement. As she closed the door behind her, she seemed to control herself with one great effort, then walking straight to the desk she said, in a broken and trembling voice, "I want you to answer me a question."

"Barbara!" said Frank, whose intended firmness had all melted away before her haggard appearance, "Barbara!" and he rose and put out his hand to draw her to him.

"Don't touch me!" she screamed, starting back. "Don't lay one finger upon me until— until you have answered my question. This morning you left this envelope on the dressing-table; tell me who is the writer and what were the contents."

She tossed an envelope on to the desk as she spoke, and leant with one hand against the wall.

"That envelope," said Frank, speaking very slowly, "is mine. I utterly deny your right to ask me any thing about it; I utterly refuse to satisfy your curiosity."

"Curiosity! it is not that; God knows it is not that feeling merely that prompts me. This is the second time you have, to my knowledge, received letters in that writing. The first time was at Bissett, when you left suddenly, immediately after its receipt. I suspected then, but had no right to ask; now I have the right, and I demand to know!"

" I can only repeat what I said before: I most positively decline to tell you."

" Beware, Frank! You ought to know me by this time; but you don't. If you don't satisfy me on this point, I leave you for ever."

" You have your answer," said Frank; " now let me get to my work."

" You still refuse?"

" You heard what I said."

She drew herself up and left the room; the next minute he heard the street-door shut, and, running to the dining-room window, saw her hail a cab and get into it.

" There's the first lesson, at all events," said he to himself. " When she comes back to dinner, she will be cooler, and more amenable to reason."

He finished his work, and walked down with it to the *Statesman* Office. On his return he found a commissionaire in the hall talking to his servant. He asked the latter where her mistress was, but the girl said she had not come in, at the same time handing him a letter.

It was very brief; it merely said:

"You have decided; and henceforth you and I never meet again. Mrs. Schröder, with whom I am staying, will send her maid for a box which I have left ready packed. I hope you may be more happy with your correspondent, and in your return to your old life, than you have been with   B. C."

As Frank Churchill read this, the lines wavered before his eyes, and he reeled against the wall.

CHAPTER XIII.

MR. SCADGERS PAYS A VISIT.

THOSE who had been most intimately acquainted with Mr. Scadgers of Newman Street had never known him under any circumstances devote a portion of his valuable time to sacrificing to the Graces. He was popularly supposed to sleep in his clothes; and as those garments were seldom entirely free from fluff or " flue," there were probably some grounds for the supposition; but he could not have slept in his big high-boots, though no one had ever seen him without them, save Jinks. Jinks had more than once seen his master with slippered feet, and trembled; for Mr. Scadgers' boots were to him what those other Ingoldsby-celebrated boots were to the Baron Ralph de Shurland, what his hair was to Sampson, what his high-heels were to Louis Quatorze. Without his boots, Mr. Scadgers was

quite a different man ; he talked of " giving time,"
of " waiting a day or two," of " holding-off a bit ;"
this was in his slippers : but when once his boots
were on, in speaking of the same debtor he told
Jinks to " sell him up slick, and clear off all his
sticks." He always seemed to wear the same suit
of black, and all the washing that he was ever
known to indulge in was by smearing himself with
the damp corner of a towel, which he kept in the
office between the chemist's bottles, one of which
held the water; while his toilette was completed
by running a pocket-comb through his close-
cropped hair, and then smoothing it down with
the palms of his hands, whisking his boots with
his red-silk pocket-handkerchief, and putting sharp
spiky points to his nails by the aid of a vicious-
looking buck-handled penknife.

Thoroughly accustomed to his patron's appearance, Jinks was, then, struck with wonderment on
beholding him one morning enter the office in com-
paratively gorgeous array. Through the folds of a
white waistcoat there protruded a large shirt-frill,
certainly of rather a yellow hue, and not so neat in

the plaits as it ought to have been, but for all that
an undeniable frill, such as adorned the breasts of
the dandies of the last generation; his usual nap-
less greasy hat had been discarded for a very elegant article in white beaver, which had apparently
been the property of some other gentleman, and
acquired by its present owner in that species of
commercial transaction known as a " swop," as it
was much too large for Mr. Scadgers, and oblite-
rated every sign of his hair, while a corner of the
red-silk pocket-handkerchief fell out gracefully
over the back of his head. In his hand Mr.
Scadgers carried one damp black-beaver glove,
and a thick stick like an elongated ruler, with a
silver top and a silk tassel. Mr. Jinks was so
overpowered at this apparition that he sat gazing
with open mouth at his master, unable to speak a
word; he had one comfort, however,—Mr. Scadgers had his boots on, so that under all this frivolity there lurked an intention of stern business.

Mr. Scadgers took no notice of his subordi-
nate's astonishment; but placing the glove and
the stick on his desk, taking off the white hat, and

having a thorough mopping with the red-silk pocket-handkerchief, looked through his letters, and proceeded to indorse them, for Jinks to answer, in his usual business way. Some of his correspondence amused him, for he smiled and shook his head at the letter in a waggish way, as though the writer were chaffing him; in glancing over another he would lay his finger alongside his nose and mutter, "No, no, my boy! not by no means, no how!" while at others his larger eye would gleam ferociously, the upper corner of his mouth would twist higher than ever, and he would shake his fist at the paper and utter words not pleasant to hear. His mental emotions did not, however, interfere with his business habits: as he finished each letter he wrote the substance of his reply on the back for Jinks to copy, drew three or four cheques, which he also handed over to his factotum, and locked away some flimsy documents which had formed the contents of certain of the letters, in his cash-box. Some of the letters received by that morning's post had contained bank-notes, and these Mr. Scadgers examined most scrupulously before putting them away, holding them between his eyes and the light to examine the water-mark, carefully scrutinising the engraving, and finally comparing the numbers, dates, and ciphers with the list contained in a printed bill pasted against the inside of his desk-lid headed "Stolen." Over one of the notes, after comparing it with this list, Mr. Scadgers chuckled vastly.

"90275 LB January 12! there you are correct to a T. I thought they'd turn up about this time. I say, Jinks, here's one of the notes as was stolen from Robarts's; you recollect? Come up from Doncaster in renewal-fee from Honourable Capting Maitland. He took it over the Leger, no doubt: they always thought at Scotland Yard that that was the way those notes would get put off; and they was right. Send this back to the capting, Jinks,—he's gone back to Leeds barracks now,—and tell him all about it; we can't have that, you know; might get us into trouble; and if he wants a renewal, he must send another. He won't know where he got it from, bless you!

reg'lar careless cove as ever was; he ain't due till Friday, and he's sent up to-day in a reg'lar fright. You must step round to Moss's and tell 'em to proceed in Hetherington's matter. There's a letter there from Sir Mordaunt, askin' for more time, and promisin' all sorts of things; but I'm sick of him and his blather. Tell Moss to put the screw on, and he'll pay up fast enough. Write a line to young Sewell, and tell him he can have 125*l.*, and the rest in madeiry. He's in Scotland; you'll find his address in the book,—Killy-something; say the wine can be sent to the Albany; but I won't do it in any other way. Any one been in this morning?"

"Only Sharp, from Parkinson's," said Mr. Jinks, who was already deep in letter-writing.

"Well," said his principal, "what did he want?"

"He came to know if you'd be in another two hundred for Mr. Beresford," replied Jinks, looking up from his work. "He's been hit at Doncaster, and wants the money most immediate."

"Then he won't get it from me," said Mr. Scadgers; "I won't have no more of his paper, at no price. He's up to his neck already, is Mr. Beresford; and that old aunt of his don't mean dying yet, from all I hear."

"There's the bishop," suggested Jinks.

"Oh, blow the bishop! He might be bled on the square, but he'd turn precious rusty if he thought it was stiff he was paying for. No, no; Master Beresford's taking lodgings in Queer Street, I fancy; Parkinson holds more of his paper than you think of, and if he wants to go deeper, he must go by himself; I won't be in it."

"All right," said Jinks; "I'll put a cross against his name in the books. Rittman's boy looked in to see if his father could have two pounds till Saturday. I told him to call again this afternoon."

"Till Saturday," said Scadgers with a grin. "You never see such a Saturday as that'll be, Jinks. Poor devil! there's nothing but the carcass left there; and he's worked well too, and brought us plenty of custom, though not of the best sort. Let the boy have a sovereign when he comes, Jinks, and tell him if his father don't pay, I'll put him in prison; not that he'll mind that one dump. Oh, by the way, give me all the paper of young Prescott's that you've got by you."

Mr. Jinks opened a large iron safe let into the wall just behind his stool, and from a drawer therein took out a bundle of tape-tied papers. From this he selected four, and as he handed them over to his principal said, " Here they are; two with Pringle, one with Compton, and one I.O.U.,—total, one seventy-five. I was going to ask you what you intended to do about them. The young feller was here yesterday wanting to see you, and looking regularly down upon his luck."

" Ah," said Scadgers, "there's something up about them, what I don't know; but I'm a-goin' on that business now. I shall be away for an hour or two, Jinks."

" You ain't a-goin' to get married, are you, Mr. Scadgers?" asked the little old man with a look of alarm; "it would never do to bring a female into the concern."

Scadgers laughed outright. "Married! no, you old fool, not I. Can't a man put on a bit of finery"—here he smoothed the yellow shirt-frill with his grimy fingers—"without your supposing there's a woman in the case? However, I'm goin' to call upon a lady, and that's the truth; but all in a matter of business. Hand over them bills of Prescott's, and don't expect me till you see me."

So saying, Mr. Scadgers took the bills from Jinks and placed them in his fat pocket-book, which he buttoned into the breast-pocket of his frock-coat, gave himself a good mopping with the red-silk pocket-handkerchief before throwing it into the big white hat, and placing that elegant article on his head, took up the one damp glove and the ruler-like stick, and went out.

A consciousness of the shirt-frill, or the hat, or both, pervaded Mr. Scadgers' mind as he walked through the streets, and gave him an air very different from that which usually characterised his business perambulations. He seemed to feel that he was calling upon the passers-by for observation and notice; and certainly the passers-by seemed to respond to the appeal. Ribald boys stuck the red-covered books of domestic household expenditure which they carried into their breasts, and swaggered by with heads erect; others openly expressed their opinion that it was " all dicky" with him; while a more impudent few suggested that he had stolen the " guv'nor's tile," or borrowed his big brother's hat; nor were the suggestions that he was a barber's clerk out for a holiday wanting on the part of the youthful populace. In an ordinary way Mr. Scadgers was thoroughly proof against the most cutting chaff: the most terrific things had been said about his boots, and he had remained adamant; drunken men had requested permission to light their pipes at his nose, and he had never winced; in allusion to his swivel-eye, boys had asked him to look round the corner and tell them what o'clock it was, without ruffling his temper in the smallest degree. But in the present instance he felt in an abnormal state; he knew that there was ground for the satire which was being poured out upon him, and he fled into the first omnibus for concealment. He rode to the utmost limits of the omnibus-journey, and when he alighted he had still a couple of miles to walk to his destination. He inquired his way, and set out manfully. The weather was magnificent; one of those early October days when, though the sun's rays are a little tempered of their burning heat, and the air has a freshness which it has not known for months, the country yet wears a summer aspect. Mr. Scadgers' way lay along a high-road, on either side of which were fields: now huge yellow patches shorn of their produce, and, while awaiting the ploughshare, looking like the clean-shaved faces of elderly gentlemen; now broken up into rich loam furrows driven through by the puffing snorting engine which has supplanted the patient Dobbin, the handle-holding labourer, and whip-cracking boy of our childhood, and against which Mr. Tennyson's Northern farmer inveighed with such bitterness. Far away on the horizon lay a broad wooded belt, broken in the centre, where two tall trees, twining their topmost branches together, formed a kind of natural arch, and beyond which one expected—absurdly enough—to find the sea. The road was quiet enough; a few carts, laden with farm-produce or manure, crept lazily along it; now and then a carrier's wagon, drawn by a heavily-trotting horse with bells on his collar, jolted by, or the trap of a town-traveller returning from the home-circuit, driven by an ill-dressed hobbledehoy with the traveller nodding by his side, and the black-leather apron strapped over the back seat, to make the trap look as much like a phaeton as possible, rattled townward. But when, in obedience to the directions on a finger-post, Mr. Scadgers turned out of the high-road up a long winding lane, fringed on either side by high hedges, on which " Autumn's fiery finger" had been laid only to increase their beauty a thousand-fold, where not a sound broke the stillness save his own footfall and the occasional chirping of the birds, he seemed for the first time to awake to the beauty of the scene. Climbing to the top bar of a gate in the hedge on the top of a little eminence, he seated himself, took off the big hat, mopped himself violently with the red-silk handkerchief, and looked round on the panorama of meadow and woodland, with tiny silver threads of water here and there interspersed, until his heart softened and he had occasion to rub the silver head of the ruler-like stick into his eyes.

" Lor' bless me !" he muttered to himself; " it's like Yorkshire, and yet prettier than that; softer and quieter like. More than twenty years since I've seen any thing like this. And poor Ann! Daisy-chains we used to make in Fairlow's mead, just like that field there, when we was little children; daisy-chains and buttercups, and——poor Ann! And to think what I'm now a-goin' to ——Lord help us! well, it *is* a rum world !" with which sage though incoherent reflections Mr. Scadgers resumed the big hat, dismounted from the gate, and continued his walk.

As he proceeded up the lane, he began to take particular notice of the objects by which he was more immediately surrounded; and on hearing the tramp of hoofs he peered through the hedge, and saw strings of horses, each mounted by its groom, at exercise. At these animals Mr. Scadgers looked with a by no means uncritical eye, and seemed satisfied, for he muttered, " Good cattle and plenty of 'em too ; looks like business that. Wise head she has; I knew it *would* turn out all right." When he arrived at the lodge, he stopped in front of the gates and looked scrutinisingly about him, then rang the bell, and stared hard but pleasantly at the buxom woman who stood curtseying with the gate in her hand. Inside, Mr. Scadgers noticed that every thing looked neat and prosperous; he did not content himself with going straight up the carriage-drive, but diverged across the lodge-keeper's garden, and peered into the little farm-yard, where the mastiff came out of his kennel to scan the stranger, and where two or three helpers, lounging on the straw-ride, or polishing bits as they leant against the stable-doors, mechanically knuckled their foreheads as he passed by. Arriving at the house, Mr. Scadgers found the front-door open ; but a

pull at the bell brought a staid, middle-aged woman (Kate Mellon, for it was The Den which Mr.
Scadgers was visiting, never could stand what
she called "flaunting hussies," as servants), by
whom he was ushered into the pretty little hall,
hung with its antlers, its foxes' brushes, and its
sporting picture, into the dining-room. There he
was left by himself to await the coming of the
owner of the house.

Now Mr. Scadgers, though by no means a
nervous or impressible man, seemed on this occasion to have lost his ordinary calm, and to be
in a very excitable state. He laid the big hat
carefully on the table, refreshed himself with a
thorough mop with the red-silk handkerchief,
and rubbed his hands through his stubbly black
hair; then he walked up and down the room,
alternately sucking the silver head of the ruler-
like stick, and muttering incoherencies to himself,
and ever and anon he would stop short in his
perambulations and glance at the door with an
air almost of fright. The door at length was
opened with a bang, and Kate Mellon entered

the room. The skirt of her dress was looped
up, and showed a pair of red-striped stockings
and large, though well-shaped, thick Balmoral
boots; she had a driving-whip in one hand and
on the other a strong dogskin gauntlet, stretched
and stained. Her face was flushed, her eyes
bright, and the end of her hair was just escap-
ing from the light knot into which it had been
bound. With a short nod to her visitor, at
whose personal appearance she gave a glance of
astonishment, she began the conversation by asking what his pleasure was.

If Mr. Scadgers' behaviour had been somewhat peculiar before her entrance, it was now
ten times more remarkable. At first he stood
stock-still with his mouth open, gazing at her
with distended eyes; then he fell to nodding his
head violently and rubbing his hands as if thoroughly delighted, and then looked her up and
down as though he were mentally appraising each
article of dress.

"What's the man up to?" said Kate, after
undergoing a minute of this inspection; "come,

none of this tomfoolery here. What do you want?"

Recalled to himself by the sharp tone in which these words were uttered, Mr. Scadgers fell into his usual state, bowed, and said he had called by appointment.

"By appointment?" said Kate; "oh, ah, I recollect now. You overcharged me for two horses and a dog in the list for last year. I filled up your form-thing fairly enough; why didn't you go by that?"

"Two horses and a dog!" repeated Mr. Scadgers. "There's some mistake, miss; my name's Scadgers."

"Lord, that is a good 'un!" said Kate, dropping the whip and clapping her hands in an ecstasy of laughter. "I thought you were the man about the taxes that I've sent for to come to me, too. So your name's Scadgers, is it? I've heard of you, sir; you get your living in a queer way."

"Pretty much the same as you and the rest of the world, I believe," said Scadgers,

pleasantly;—"by the weakness of human na-
tur'!"

"Which you take a pretty considerable advantage of, eh?"

"Well, I don't know: a gent wants money
and he hears I've got it, and he comes to me
for it. I don't seek him,—he seeks me; I tell
him what he'll have to pay for it, and he agrees.
He has the money and he don't return it; and
when he goes through the Court and it all comes
out, people cry, 'Oh, Scadgers again! oh, the
bloodsucker! here's iniquity!' and all the rest
of the gammon. If people wants luxuries, miss,
they must pay for 'em, as you know well
enough."

This was not said in the least offensively, but
in a quiet earnest manner, as though the man had
real belief in what he stated, and saw no harm in
the calling he was defending. Kate, who had a
pretty shrewd knowledge of character, saw this at
once, and felt more kindly disposed to her new
acquaintance than she had at first.

"Well," she said, "what's sauce for the goose

is sauce for the gander, they say; and it's not my business to preach to you, and you wouldn't heed it if I did. I got you to come here on business. You hold some acceptances of Mr. James Prescott's."

"That's true, miss; I've got 'em here in my pocket-book."

"What's the amount?"

"The total, one seventy-five; cab-hire and loss of time, say one seventy-five ten six."

"Hand them over, and I'll write you a cheque."

"Well," said Mr. Scadgers, slowly, "we don't generally take cheques in these matters,—it ain't business; they mightn't be paid, you know,—but I don't mind doing it for you."

Something in the tone of this last sentence which struck oddly on Kate Mellon's ear,—a soft tender tone of almost parental affection; a tone which seemed to bring back memory of past days. She looked up hurriedly, but Mr. Scadgers' swivel-eye was fixed on the wall above her head; and in the rest of his countenance there was no more emotion visible than on the face of a Dutch clock. Kate Mellon took out her desk and wrote the cheque.

"There!" she said, handing it to him,— "there's your money; hand over the bills. All right! Now, two things more. One, you'll swear never to let Mr. Prescott know who paid this money. Good! The other, if ever he comes to you for help again—I don't think he will, mind; but if he does—you'll refuse him, and let me know."

"That's what they all say," said Mr. Scadgers, "' if they come again, refuse 'em;' and they do come again, and I don't refuse 'em,—that is if I think they're good for the money,—but I'll swear I'll do it for you."

"I believe you," said Kate, simply. "Now, have some lunch before you go."

"No, thank you," said Scadgers, "no lunch; but I should like a glass of wine to drink your health in."

"You shall have it, and welcome," said she, ringing the bell; "and I'll have one with you, for I was at the dumb-jockey business when you came in, and it rather takes it out of one."

When the wine was brought, Kate filled two glasses, and, taking up one, nodded to Mr. Scadgers. "Here's luck," said she, shortly. Mr. Scadgers took his glass, and said: "The best of luck to you in every thing, and God bless you, my— miss, I mean! And now, I've heard a lot about your stable and place—would you mind my going round them, before I go?"

"Mind!" said Kate; "I'll take you myself." And they walked into the farm together.

"It was as much as I could do," said Mr. Scadgers to himself, as, half an hour afterwards, he walked down the lane on his way back to town —"it was as much as I could do to prevent throwing my arms round her neck and telling her all about it. What a pretty creetur' it is; and what spirit! I suppose she's nuts on young Prescott, and they'll be gettin' married. Lord! that would be a rum start if he ever knew—but he won't know, nor any of 'em; we shall never let on. Woman of business too; keeps accounts I noticed, when she opened her desk; and all the place in such order; kept as neat as a drawing-room those stables. Well, that's one thing you did right, John Scadgers, and one you won't be sorry for some day."

"That's a queer customer," said Kate to herself, as she stood in the lane by the lodge-gate, looking after his receding figure. "A very queer customer. What a grip he gave my hand when he said good-by! My fingers ache with it still. And there was no nonsense about him; I could see that in a minute. Where have I seen him before? I've some sort of recollection of him, but I can't fit it to any thing particular—he's not in the horse-line, and he's not a swell; so I don't see where I can have come across him. Glad he looked in this morning, for I was precious dull: I can't make out what this weight is that's hanging over me for the last few days, just as though something was going to happen. I think another glass of Madeira would do me good; but I promised Simnel I'd knock that off. I wonder what's come of Simnel for the last few days. That old Scadgers seemed to know something about this place, noticed the alterations in the five-acre meadow; and when I asked him, said he remembered the place when it was Myrtle Farm. I must ask Simnel about him, he—Lord, how depressed and stupid I feel again!" She turned back and fastened the gate after her. One of the gatekeeper's chubby children came running out to meet her, and she caught the little thing up in her arms, and carried it into the lodge. As she was putting it down she heard the tramp of horses' feet, and raising her head, looked through the window. The next instant her cheeks flushed scarlet; she dropped the child into a chair, and rushing to the gate, threw it open, and stood gazing down the road.

Yes, it was he! no mistaking his figure, even if she had not recognised the horse. It was he riding so close to the lady by his side, bending over her and looking down into her upturned face. So pre-occupied that he never even bestowed a glance upon the place so well known to him, so frequently visited in bygone days. And she, who was she? Kate could see that she was slim, could see her fair hair gathered in a knot beneath her hat,—it must be the woman of whom Simnel had spoken. And Kate Mellon gave a loud groan, and clenched her nails into the palms of her hands, and stood looking after them with quivering lips and a face as pale as death.

Just at that moment two grooms came riding round the corner, side by side. The sound of their horses' feet recalled Kate to herself. She looked up, and in one of them recognised Beresford's man. She collected herself by a great effort, and beckoned to him. The man saw her, touched his hat, and rode up at once, leaving his companion to proceed by himself.

"William," said Kate, "who's that lady riding with your master?"

"Mrs. Schröder, miss; Saxe-Coburg Square. Mr. Schröder drives pair of chestnuts, miss, in mail-phcayton, plain black harness. May have noticed 'em; often in the Park, miss."

"Ah! No; I think not. Schröder,—Saxe-Coburg Square, you said?"

"Yes, miss. Beg pardon, miss," added the man, who had himself been formerly in Kate's service, and by whom, as by all of his fraternity, she was adored,—beg pardon, miss; but nothing wrong, is there? You're looking uncommon ill, miss."

"No," said Kate, with a ghastly smile. "I'm all right, thank you, William. Good-day! ride on!" and William, touching his hat, clapped spurs to his horse, and rode off.

That night the mail-cart was waiting outside the little village post-office, and the old woman was just huddling the letters into the bag, when a groom came up at a hand-gallop, and dismounting, gave in a letter, saying,

"Just in time, Mrs. Mallins, I think!"

The old woman peered at him over her spectacles.

"Oh, it's you, Thomas, is it? Well, I'll take a letter from your mistress, though I'm not bound to do it by the reg'lations. You're after time, Thomas."

"I know, Mrs. Mallins; but Miss Kate said 'twere most particular. And I were to tell you so, and—"

"Air you comin' with that bag?" growled the mail-cart driver, putting his head into the shop.

"All right, my man! all right!" said the old lady, handing him the bag. "There it is. Thomas, you can tell your lady she was in time."

Half an hour afterwards Kate Mellon's servant looked into the dining-room. There was no light, and she was about to withdraw, when she heard her mistress's voice say, "What is it?"

"Oh, nothing, ma'am; only Thomas says the letter was in time."

"Very well," said Kate. Then, when the door was shut again, she muttered between her clenched teeth: "It's done now, and can't be undone! Now, Master Charley, look out for yourself!"

END OF VOL. II.

www.ingramcontent.com/pod-product-compliance
Lightning Source LLC
Chambersburg PA
CBHW020925120726
47905CB00008B/2384